T0102818

Beyond the Arc

There's a Place Called Auralee

Fred Mitchell

Order this book online at www.trafford.com
or email orders@trafford.com

Most Trafford titles are also available at major online book retailers.

© Copyright 2010 Fred Mitchell.
All rights reserved. No part of this publication may be reproduced, stored in a retrieval
system, or transmitted, in any form or by any means, electronic, mechanical, photocopying,
recording, or otherwise, without the written prior permission of the author.

Printed in Victoria, BC, Canada.

ISBN: 978-1-4269-0312-0 (soft)
ISBN: 978-1-4269-0314-4 (ebook)

*Our mission is to efficiently provide the world's finest, most comprehensive
book publishing service, enabling every author to experience success.
To find out how to publish your book, your way, and have it available
worldwide, visit us online at www.trafford.com*

Trafford rev. 2/5/2010

Trafford
PUBLISHING® www.trafford.com

North America & international
toll-free: 1 888 232 4444 (USA & Canada)
phone: 250 383 6864 ♦ fax: 250 383 6804

DEDICATION

To my wife of 57 years, Shirley, goes my heartfelt thanks for her patience and truly great editing job...I dedicate this book to her.

Scotland

CONTENTS

PROLOGUE

TODAY IS Friday, March 16th, 2008. My name is Fred Mitchell and my world consists of stuff instantaneously beamed to me via satellite television or by my daily news rag. Perhaps I am a bit cynical of those folks, who by their proclaimed investigative prowess and intellect, bring to me reports of every time some celebrity hic-cups or is arrested for the umpteenth time on a DUI charge. Adding to my misery are their steady dissertations about any and all murders, rapes, disasters, pedophilia, opinions concerning everyone's rights (except my own), and *Lordy, Lordy,* let's hear it again on O. J. Simpson's and Britney Spears' latest travesties. No wonder many of today's youth have become so alienated from reality that they could not identify the states next door to where they live, name our last president, or for that matter some probably could not tell you the name of our current president.

Born in 1983 I am twenty-five years of age, six feet tall, 185 pounds, sport a neatly trimmed mustache and beard, brown eyes, dark complexion, and have a distinctive voice that is deemed pleasant and always recognizable.

I am a graduate from a leading Illinois university where I earned my master's degree, have worked since graduation with a major advertising firm in Chicago, make a good salary, potentially have a good future ahead of me, and live in a nice apartment in a western suburb.

My best friend and business associate is Kenneth H. Effington who works for the same firm. Ken is a mellow, trustworthy fellow who tends to imbibe perhaps a bit more than he should. He says it helps him relax and escape the tedious tensions of today's rat race. Ken stands 5' 10", 170 pounds, has dark sandy hair, hazel eyes, neatly trimmed mustache, and small freckles adorn his cheeks. He is sometimes passive, but most importantly, always fun to be with.

My family consists of my father, William (Bill, the informed, b.1953), my mother, Rebecca (Becky, the loving, b.1955), and my three siblings, John (the inquisitor, b.1976), Sue Ellen (the caring, b.1978), and Barbara, (the brat, b.1980). As for me? I was called the crusader because, as the youngest, I was always chasing rainbows. Further, I was the only member of my family who obtained a college degree, not to mention a master's degree. I managed to accomplish this through scholastic scholarship awards, educational loans, working hard during the off season, and working at the university cafeteria during the school year.

Obtaining a college education was a daunting task; however, since graduation I have paid off all my loans. There is a bit of jealousy that occasionally surfaces with a couple of my siblings, but mom and dad are always proud of most anything I do.

I have been seriously involved for some time with a lovely debutant, Samantha Theodora Pierson, 22 years of age, five-feet-five, 107 pounds, shoulder length dark brown hair, piercing brown eyes, lovely shape, and a smile that is quite mesmerizing. She commands the center of attention whenever she is present and is a socially accepted member of the "in-group." I have come to realize this presents me with some problems…. I am rather a loner, certainly not at all antisocial, but I need my private turf and want it to belong to me. Also, I am rather disposed to be more in tune with what has gone before than with what may come later, and enjoy small groups away from the hassle of the hectic pace of today.... These little conflicts will bare watching.

****

At 5:30 AM each Monday through Friday I start my weekly ritual, catch the 7:45 commuter to Chicago, arrive at the office at 9:00, say hello to fellow workers, open my morning mail, and check my calendar for meetings or appointments. Next comes lunch, a quick sandwich and a soft drink, usually in my office delivered by my faithful secretary, Shirley. Finally at 4:45 PM it is time to begin my Monday through Friday evening rituals, a choreography of events that never seem to change.

I rush to catch the five o'clock commuter train for the suburbs, purchase a newspaper from a young man who calls me Mr. Fred, give him a 25 cent tip, purchase a canned martini, and take my usual seat.

Usually on Fridays I arrive at my station at 6:15, jump in my car, hurry home, consume a quick cup of canned soup with a Diet Cola, take a shower, redress in my suit, and prepare myself for another "exciting" evening with Sam at her country club.

As I arrive Samantha is waiting in her doorway, a remarkable lovely lady. All the young, and some not so young, wolves think so too. Sam revels in their attention! I am not a jealous person, but I get somewhat irked at having to scramble for a little undivided attention from her. I know she means well, but she has some growing up to do. Sometimes I join Ken at the bar and just let the evening slide by until gratefully time arrives to take Sam home.

Tonight she flattered me saying what a wonderful evening it had been. (Her definition, I assure you.) At 1:00 AM we arrived at her door and she said, "Fred, you are so gallant and I love you for it. Don't ever change." I kissed her gently (perhaps gallantly), said, "Goodnight, Sam. I'll pick you up before lunch tomorrow for Bridge at the club."

As I finished getting ready for bed it was 2:00 AM; while standing in front of the mirror…the image looking back at me seemed to say, *"Air ye haven fun?"* I thought for a moment and answered, "Yeh, think so…maybe."

I lay awake for some time thinking about my response to a manifestation which I thought was staring at me from within the mirror. *Really*, I told myself, and finally drifted off into a restless slumber thinking, *Fred, something is wrong with the equation which governs your life.*

During the night, although sleeping well, I experienced a very unusual dream…. It was as if I were in a place not of this world and I awoke perspiring, trying to imagine that my illusion might return, but it had faded forever into memory. A very haunting dream yet not an unpleasant one. There also was a melody with words. An enchanting tune which along with my dream alluded recall.

CHAPTER 1

THE RAT RACE

SATURDAY MORNING was not unusual for this time of year, rainy and cool. I dressed myself accordingly, went for my usual weekend jog through the overcast on my three mile run which took me through a lovely nearby park. On a nicer day it would have been a delight to see the sun rising and the birds singing to welcome me, but not today. It was 8:00 AM and in two hours I would pick Sam up for another "festive" day at the club. I said to myself, *Well anyway, it'll be warm and dry.*

****

We left Sam's place, arrived at the club, and at 11:00 AM lunched. At one o' clock we adjourned to the card room where the next four hours would be devoted to Duplicate Bridge. After enduring a dull and lackluster effort, all I could say was we occupied space at the table. Sam had spent more of her time conversing with our opponents about social events than she did about bidding and playing her cards. We got what we deserved! We were dead last and that didn't bother Sam at all, but it irked me. I am just not pleased with being last at anything. For a very brief moment the thought, *something wrong with this equation,* once again flashed through my mind. However, I just smiled and told Sam how much I had enjoyed playing Bridge with her.... *What the hell is this? I lied! What in the world am I doing to myself?*

We left the card room for the cocktail lounge. I felt like maybe at least two drinks before dinner might be in order. Finally we were alone and ole naive me thought we might enjoy a few moments of private conversation. But that feeling disappeared quickly. Soon a line of Sam's acquaintances, both male and female, began to file by. Some of them recognized me and some had no idea what role I played in this drama.

****

On schedule we adjourned to the dining room, were seated at a table for six, and as Sam had planned it, we were the center couple. On the way to our table I am sure Sam spoke to or waved at everyone in sight. Soon we were joined by two couples, one of whom I had not yet met. Once again I began to feel like baggage just along for filler, where a male companion was needed.

My first martini, the others had wine, was served; almost immediately the conversation raced into self indulgent accolades of the two gentlemen's business acumens.... To me it was really boring stuff. Ralph, the one I had never met, turned to me and in an authoritarian voice said, "And, Red, how did you come by the name Red and what, Sir, do you do for a living?".... After due thought I answered, "Well, Ralph, when I was born my skin was a very bright red. The hospital staff referred to me as Red and the name stuck. As for a living, I am President of HATS (Holes and That Stuff, International), and our company logo is a Derby. And, Sir, we dig the finest outhouse holes and construct the best privies in the world. Our motto is *Bottoms on Display*." I lifted my glass to him and he was thunderstruck, which is how I wished him to be.

We had not yet ordered our dinner when I excused myself. I said I had received an urgent call on my cell phone from a client that required my immediate attention and would return as soon as it was practical.

After I left Ralph turned to Sam and said, "Samantha, is he for real?" She glanced quickly at him and replied, "Oh, yes, he is very much for real." This left Ralph even further perplexed.

I returned to the table after a lengthy absence, during which time they had eaten, to say my goodbyes. I took Sam's arm saying, "Let's go." On the way home it came to me, *The answer to my equation became clear.* When we arrived at her door I kissed her, said it was my hope she had a good time, was sorry to have missed dinner, and said goodnight.

By now my feelings of how I fit into Sam's life suddenly had became more evident. I said to myself, *Fred, you know this has got to stop, and soon. Sam is beautiful, is from a wealthy family, and is pleasant to be with when you are alone with her. Ah, herein is a piece of the equation…I am seldom alone with her. I believe that in her way she truly loves me, and am never in want for a good, if not boring, time…but she is vane, selfish, and bossy.* All these were pieces of the puzzle which I could not much longer endure.

Sunday morning arrived, a nice day. Having nothing better to do I decided to go for a drive out to the countryside. I needed time to think…my mind was far away…. A half hour later something huge was coming straight at me, a semi-truck was on my side of the road or was I was on his, screeching tires, blaring horns, and suddenly unearthly silence…. Numbness overtook me; it felt as though my mind was somewhere outside my body. There was no pain. I felt lucid but realized something unusual was happening. Perhaps only a bad dream that would soon pass.

****

Monday morning arrived and things still didn't seem right; however, I couldn't get a handle on what was wrong. After acquiring a hot cup of coffee and boarding my commuter train, I sat watching familiar scenery rush by. My mind seemed a muddle and all of a sudden I realized yesterday was missing. *Sunday was gone*! I could not remember anything about Sunday except leaving for a drive in the country. I tried to focus on yesterday, but it was as though my mind refused to go there. I thought, *Oh, heck, Fred, eventually memory will come back.*

While walking the two blocks to my office, I met Ken, said, "Morning, Ken, hope you had a good weekend. Come on up to my office, say at 9:30, for a little conference. I'll have coffee brought in." Ken was quick to respond, "You are on, ole buddy, and I'd like a doughnut."

When Ken arrived I poured us each a cup of coffee, sat back in my chair and unloaded. "Ken, tell me, are you having fun? Is life going the way you hoped it would?" He relaxed for a moment, sighed, took a huge bite from his doughnut, and looked intently at me before replying…. "Hell no, I'm not!…. Now that you have asked me, what the hell did you have in mind?"

I wasn't surprised by his response and countered, "Well, old friend, it is comforting to know you feel the same as I do. Yes, I do have a suggestion," sat back in my chair, looked seriously at Ken and said, "You know we both have accrued some vacation days, so why don't we take a three week trip. I have an idea, if you are amenable to it.

"Let's take a vacation to the Highlands of Scotland. I know of an old Inn at Penoaken, which today stands very much as it did a couple hundred years ago. We could hunt grouse, play some golf, enjoy the area's history, and for awhile just go wherever and do whatever we want. What do you think?"

After a few moments of meditation, Ken replied, "Hey, Fred, not bad. Don't know a fiddlers damn about grouse hunting but I guess they could teach us anything we needed to know." I agreed, especially since both of us had learned to use shotguns in our youth.

We chose the dates May 9th through May 30th and submitted our requests which were confirmed up-the-line by our department heads. Thereafter I immediately placed a call to the Travis Inn at Penoaken in Scotland and booked reservations for two rooms for the above dates.

Literature which followed described the Inn and the area surrounding it as being in a forested meadow at the edge of the village. The Inn was built in 1739, although modernized, it still remained very much as it did in 1739. The village of Penoaken was residence to several homes of that era, to the village church, rebuilt in 1709, and a small museum of that period.

There were remote areas nearby where grouse hunting should be excellent in May. The Inn was owned and managed by Henry Travis and had been in his family since 1790.

****

I continued to experience recurring thoughts about my missing Sunday. It bothered me that I could still not remember anything specific about that day. But as time moved on I began to think less and less about it and we continued to refine our plans to visit Scotland.

One evening at the club I broke the news about my upcoming vacation to Samantha. She was visibly upset, asking how I could do such a thing without consulting her first? I reminded her, much to her consternation, that we were not married, and as such were free to go where we pleased and do what we wanted so long as it was morally and ethically OK.

Sam wasn't at all moved by my explanation and I said to her, "Take a couple of days to think about it." I didn't intend this to affect our situation, but we both needed to get beyond bickering. It was time she understood my need to be away from my job would be in both our best interests.

Sam tried to pull out all of the stops with her crying act but I firmly interjected, "No! No! Sam, that won't help." We have a date for next Saturday and Sunday at the club, and unless I hear otherwise from you it's still on." Finally Sam decided the "hurt act" wasn't working and she smiled, said, "Of course it is on, Fred. I'll be alright."

Later when I took her home I said, "Goodnight, Sam, I love you. I have got to get away from the rat race for awhile, and hope to return rejuvenated and with a new outlook on life. Three weeks isn't a lifetime." She smiled, a rather hurt smile. It was evident her ego was still smarting and she said, "Yes, Fred, I guess I understand. I love you too."

Three days passed with no response from Sam. I wasn't going to take the lead on this so I waited and finally Sam called. It was a relief when she said, " Fred, I have thought a lot about what you said, and want you to know, it's OK what you are doing. I need you to be happy and will miss you. Go ahead with my blessings." I was taken aback. *Was this Sam speaking?* But before I had time to answer, she added, "*I only hope the trip serves to clear up your thinking.*" Oops, wasn't sure just what that meant, but it sounded to me like I was doing something wrong; however, I responded, "Thank you, Sam," and let it go at that.

The following weekend passed relatively peaceful as did the next couple of weeks. Sam and I spoke as little as possible of my upcoming journey. As each week passed it seemed a carbon copy of the one before. Work, commute, social events, bridge, dancing, and golf. It seemed that there were only two things in life which really mattered…work and the country club…. *Yuk!*

Ken and I, spent many hours discussing every aspect of our trip. We were both excited and wished time would hurry up. As the days slid on we continued to revise our agenda. Besides grouse hunting and golf we would visit various historical places of which there were a multitude including possibly Loch Ness, where we hoped to see *Nessie*.

Scottish lore had always fascinated me and now I would be able to soak it up. Ken was very into our plans and that was comforting to me. This needed to be a joint venture and it was becoming one.

Suddenly it was the first of May, only a few more days and we would be winging our way across the Atlantic. The first international trip for us both. On the last weekend before we left Sam and I, in our usual roles, dined at the club. However, tonight was noticeably different. Sam paid more attention to me. We danced several times and it seemed she was seeking some assurance from me that I would be returning. *It was as if she had a premonition.* I assured her that I would come back.

For some time I had been having reservations about our future, but wasn't sure what the future would now dictate. This trip was to be a chance for me for me to think-on-it. At times my relationship with Sam had been tender, warm and intimate, other times, cool, distant and impassionate.

I opted, "Sam, when I return, we will sneak off someplace for a lost weekend together, just the two of us. We'll have an unfettered opportunity to talk to each other seriously about many things, something we often seem to have difficulty doing. How does that sound, Sam?"

Sam immediately smiled, "Oh, yes, Fred. It sounds like a splendid idea. By all means let's do it." She seemed genuinely pleased; her expression showed that. I replied, "OK, Sam, I'll take care of the arrangements as soon as I return form Scotland."

This evening when we arrived at her home, we remained in the car for a few minutes and kissed passionately. Damn, she could be all woman when she wanted to be. Finally, I broke it off saying, "Sam, best we leave this right here until my return. I love you, Sam." We walked to the door without further words. As she entered the house, it was as if a harbinger had arrived to give her notice of things to come. I was certain she was shaking. I said, "Goodnight, Sam," closed the door and left.

CHAPTER 2

FROM CHICAGO TO PENOAKEN, SCOTLAND

M AY 10TH, the day of our flight from Chicago to Edinburgh, Scotland, was finally here. After arrival at Edinburgh we would secure a car, drive to the Village of Penoaken, and locate the Travis Inn.

We were traveling light, just two large suitcases, and each of us would have a carry-on. All of our hunting gear was to be provided by the Inn; if we needed anything more we would purchase it.

Our limousine arrived and we were on our way to O'Hare Field. Our baggage check-in went smoothly and security was cleared without a hitch. Ken and I hoped all this good luck was an omen of continued good fortune. There was a two hour wait until our departure. To pass time we just talked. We hoped the weather would be great, that our work back home wouldn't pile up, and would anyone miss us? We laughed about the latter.…. There was little doubt they wouldn't and the feeling would be mutual. I pondered, *Was work disinterest another missing link from my equation?*

****

When the time arrived to board our flight we took our seats and an interesting thought crossed my mind, *Why am I going to the Highlands of Scotland?* Suddenly, after all our preparations, this trip didn't seem to have a defined purpose. Yet I was compelled to go. *But why* grouse hunting? Interesting, but at this moment it seemed to be an excuse to get away from something. Was it Samantha? My work? The rat race? Or perhaps a combination of them all? It seemed there should be more? Fortunately when the captain announced our clearance for takeoff those thoughts left my mind and enthusiasm for our venture returned.

Soon we were racing down the runway and the great ship pushed it's nose into the air; we were airborne and after reaching our cruising altitude of 37,000 feet the captain turned off our seatbelt sign. We were free to move about. I turned to Ken and said, "Well, ole buddy, we are on our way. I'll buy us a martini and then we should get a little rest." Ken spontaneously accepted my offer.

Shortly the flight attendant, a neat, pleasant, "older lady" of I would guess about thirty-five, arrived and took our order. We were pleasantly surprised when in only a very few minutes she was back with our libations. We graciously accepted them, each took a sip, leaned back for our eight-hour journey to Edinburgh.

I turned to Ken and said, "You don't have a steady girlfriend, just a field player, huh?" He replied, "Oh, come on, Fred. You know I have tried, but it just seems they keep slipping away. Perhaps they sense my lack of a dedicated interest. I just run hot and cold and never really offer a sense of caring." I retorted, "Hey, buddy, maybe you'll find a bonnie highland lass who meets your calling." He just looked at me, smiled, and said, "Oh, sure I will." I replied, "Well, who knows? In the mystic hills of ole Scotland, who knows?"

After a couple more sips from his martini, Ken said in a rather relaxed and mellow tone, "You know, Fred, at times I have had my reservations about this sojourn, but now that we are on our way I am really anxious to get on with it. Perhaps it is the history and lore of this ancient country that seems to invigorate my imagination." At first I was taken aback by Ken's sudden interest, but I was very pleased and said, "Ken, great, I am sure we can find many things to excite and stimulate us." We raised our glasses and in a chorus, clinked them together and said, "You bet we can."

An hour whizzed by after takeoff. We finished our drink, returned our glasses to the flight attendant, and ordered dinner, steaks with all the trimmings. They were every bit as good as the steaks offered up by the country club.

After dinner to our good fortune we were soon out like lights and when we awoke it was morning and beginning to show signs of daylight. It was now May 11th. Both of us visited the lavatory and rinsed the sleep from our eyes. We were excited and soon breakfast was served: scrambled eggs, ham, fried potatoes, toast, butter, jam, and coffee. We agreed it was a sumptuous way to start our first day out from the States.

Shortly the coast of the British Isles appeared in the distance and grew more defined as each minute passed. We were just north of Ireland, so I imagined we were looking at the Scottish coastline. At an altitude of about 30,000 feet we couldn't determine many land features.

Over the intercom the captain announced we had started a slow decent into Edinburgh International Airport. Ken and I looked at each other and offered ourselves each a high-five. I said, "Wish we were already at the Inn." Ken grinned and replied, "Yep, me too, but I'm sure the drive to Penoaken will be interesting."

We relaxed and watched the scenery slowly glide past. The captain announced our altitude was now 10,000 feet. Details of the rivers, pastures, mountains, and villages were now clearly evident to us, and what a magnificent vista they presented. Seeing all this for the first time enhanced our excitement and anticipation.

Suddenly the flight attendant announced we were on final approach and to please return all seats and trays to their upright positions, fasten seatbelts, and all cell phones and other electronic devices must be turned off at this time.

Lower and lower our plane gradually settled until the landing gear gently touched the tarmac, tires squealed, and we finally rolled to a stop in front of the gate. Ken turned to me and said, "Great job, hope everything is this easy." Soon we began deplaning. My heart was beating a little faster than usual. I was plain excited. We hurried to our baggage carousel, C-8, and in just a few moments our luggage appeared.

So far, so good, and I reasoned Edinburgh International was a far cry from the crowds at O'Hare. Quickly we collected our bags and moved to the rental car counter which was nearby. Once more service was great. Our car was ready and waiting for us at curbside. We both signed a form which indicated we could drive a car with the driving position on the right side. (Ken and I had taken lessons twice to make certain we knew the ropes.)

Fortunately we were near what we would call the interstate; thus, it was possible to exit the metro area very quickly and as we did the scenery rapidly took on a rural setting. We began passing pastures, farms, and wooded areas. Mountains (munros) appeared in the distance and the ground became much more rolling with small to medium size hills. I remarked, "We are finally here, the distance to Penoaken is 100 km or about 60 miles." Allowing for a short snack break and some scenery stops, I assessed that we should be to Penoaken in about two hours.

As we continued, we stopped several times for photo-ops. The scenery was pristine and breathtaking, the air clear and cool, and our medium weight sweaters felt just right. The lochs (lakes) we passed were so beautiful and white fluffy clouds and gracious green trees framed all this splendor. The sun was brilliant, cast majestic rays onto the munros, and bounced their way across the rippling lochs. Pollution was noticeably absent. It seemed as we neared Penoaken, the more civilization receded. I mentioned to Ken it was a nice change; he nodded his agreement.

A roadway sign flashed, announcing Penoaken exit 2 km. My heart skipped a beat and as we exited another sign gave notice, Penoaken 3 km. We were almost there. Penoaken was a small village of barely 700 population; thus, locating the Travis Inn would be easy.

Upon entering the village we noticed a rather large building off the main road to our left snuggled between two hills which were covered with large pine trees. A sign at the entrance read Travis Inn at Penoaken. We both hollered, "Yea," turned and followed a stone paved lane leading to the Inn. To our right was a small loch where white swans, geese, and various colored ducks were swimming and flitting about in the calm, clear waters. Near the Inn was a small dock where a couple of canoes and a rowboat were docked; flower beds and neatly trimmed hedges completed this idyllic picture. Ken and I both remarked we had for certain arrived in old Scotland.

****

We parked the car and there she stood, the Travis Inn at Penoaken, certainly vintage eighteenth century. Built of stone it was two stories high with white wooden shutters and a steeple adorned each end of the roof. The entrance was impressive by its own right, a huge archway which featured a massive wooden door.

We entered the Inn and to our front was a reception lounge where a young lady dressed in early Scottish attire was in attendance. She was a pleasant young lady of about my age, slender, five-foot-six, 110 pounds, light blonde hair, blue eyes, and a delightful Scottish accent. You liked this girl immediately. As we approached she said, "Welcome, ye gentlemen, to the Travis Inn at Penoaken. My name is Lori and how may I be o' help to ye?"

I smiled and replied, "Hello, Lori, my name is Fred Mitchell and this is Ken Effington from Chicago, USA." In an instant she smiled and with a lilt in her answer she replied, "Oh, aye, Sirs. We be expecten ye and your rooms, numbers 102 and 103, be ready for ye occupancy. Will thee be taken dinner wi' us this evening?" I replied we would and 7:30 would be good for us. She answered, "That will be fine," and we signed for our rooms. A young man in a kilted uniform approached and said, "Gentlemen, please follow me. I willa tak' ye to your rooms."

As he was leaving I tried to tip him. He responded, "Oh, thank ye kindly, Sir, but tha' nah be required." He then gave us a hearty smile and departed. Now I was very impressed and later found out all gratuities were included in our fare as were breakfasts.

On the way to our rooms, not surprisingly, Ken noticed a small bar named *The Pub* just outside the dining room. He suggested we stop for a draft and I graciously accepted his invitation. We continued on to our rooms, unpacked, and then headed for *The Pub*. We entered and took a seat. We couldn't help but notice the magnificent antique wooden bar with a great mirror behind it. It was manned by a jolly, portly, red-headed man of about 6 feet, 210 pounds, called Scotty.

With a wide-angle smile he said, "Afternoon, gents, wha' caan I get ye?" Ken was fast to reply, "Sir, my name is Ken and this is Fred. We just arrived from the states, and we'll each have a pint of your finest Scottish ale, please." Scotty replied, "Sirs, it will be me pleasure to serve ye." He then drew a couple of giant IPA,

Maclay's India Pale Ales, from a large wooden keg and gently placed them before us saying, "Aye gentlemen, tis Scotland's finest."

They looked enticing, well even better than enticing, with their majestic foamy heads. We hoisted them graciously, clicked them together, and officially christened our arrival at Penoaken. "Here's to the Highlands of ole Scotland, and to many more of these." The foam maintained it's shape quite some time, and we managed a bit of it onto my beard and Ken's mustache. Scotty just laughed and said, "Here! Here!"

****

We left the *Pub* and came face-to-face with a rather large statue of who else but William Wallace, the reining hero of Scotland, who during the years 1297-1304 fought several vicious battles with King Edward of England for the control of Scotland. Mounted on a wall around the statue were a broadsword, a quiver, and arrows from the same period.

Next to them was a great fireplace with leather chairs and couch in front of it. One might relax here on a cool evening and allow the ghosts of Scottish lore to overwhelm you. I was certain a lot of history resided here. History's presence was all around us and told Ken of my feelings. He answered, "Hell yes, Fred, I sense it's omnipresence too. How wonderfully weird this is. Sure ain't Chicago!"

We began our inspection of the Inn's twenty some acres of grounds and gardens. At the loch we boarded a row boat and paddled around it's waters. The banks were covered in places with reeds which were home to several bird varieties. Two large white swans honked their welcome at our passing, anticipating a handout. They appeared to enjoy our presence and stayed near us for the duration of our visit as if they were escorting us through their domain. The air was clear, as was the water. Everything was so invigorating, a far cry from Chicago.

At last we docked our boat and continued our walk about the grounds. We came upon a small meadow surrounded by stately Oak and Pine trees. Ken was the first to notice what appeared to be two grave markers, very old and weathered. The inscriptions were unreadable but a marker by their side of a more recent vintage said, *Known only to God*....

Later at the Lodge we inquired of Lori and she explained, "Legend tells us that in the year 1298 duren the battle of Falkirk with English troops a young Scottish soldier was seriously wounded by a blow from an English broadsword and had to be taken from the field. He had been a staunch participant in several preceden skirmishes and was commended personally by William Wallace for his repeated acts of loyalty and bravery.

"The young soldier was instructed to return to his home which was not far from Penoaken to recover. When he arrived there he found his home burned and his parents both killed by King Edward's soldiers, an act not uncommon in that time. The lad searched for his sweetheart until she was found living with an elderly couple. Legend has it that they were taken into custody by English troops and tortured in a vain effort to extract information about William Wallace, his intentions, and his whereabouts.

"Even as he was forced to witness the repeated rapes of his sweetheart until she died, he remained silent until he finally broke and screamed, 'God save William Wallace and God condemn King Edward to burn for all eternity in Hell.' Immediately the English forced a red hot poker down the young man's throat and he was thrown while still alive into a ditch along side the body of his devastated and mutilated sweetheart. Later their bodies were disinterred and brought to Penoaken to forever rest together amongst the trees."

Lori continued, "Only history and God know their names, but every year the village holds a remembrance to their magnificent sacrifices…. We and Scotland shall never forget." We thanked Lori, I turned to Ken and said, "Getting better by the minute?" He replied, "Yep, can't wait to see what lurks around the next corner or over the next hill."

I suggested we retire to our rooms and relax for a short while before dinner which was scheduled for 7:30. Ken said, "OK, but I'll be at *The Pub* at 7:00, ole buddy, should you care to join me." I nodded my head and left.

****

Earlier I had asked Lori to make an appointment with Henry Travis for our grouse hunt instructions. We also planned to visit some historic places in Penoaken such as the old church rebuilt in 1709 and a small museum chucked full of old artifacts and lore from the eighteenth century and earlier. Even some, I understood, from the era of William Wallace.

CHAPTER 3

A DAY AT PENOAKEN

THE MORNING of May 12th arrived. We hurriedly dressed for breakfast which consisted of two three minute eggs in egg cups, goat cheese, which I had never tried before and rather liked, a slice of ham, delicate Scottish biscuits, and last but not least, strong highland coffee, a real day starter.

After our repast we sent our best wishes to the chef and were ready to begin our tour of Penoaken's historic places. However, before we left I met Henry Travis, owner of the Travis Inn. His appearance was friendly, about five-foot- ten, 185 pounds, dark brown hair, and brown eyes.

He seemed genuinely interested in us and what we had to say. I felt as though he was someone who could be trusted. For some unknown reason I had a feeling someday this might be important to us.

****

Ken and I left the Inn and strolled the half mile to the Museum at Penoaken which first opened in 1823. The curator was "Mac" McFarlane who had been on site since 1959. We were advised there wasn't much about this area or of the museum's contents that Mac was not familiar with. Wearing his red and green checkered kilts, Mac greeted us. He had a healthy gray beard, sported a great smile, and looked every bit the proper Scot. "Greetings, and welcome to the Museum at Penoaken; I be expecten ye and will be taken ye on a tour of our facility." I answered, "Thank you, Sir, we are anxious to visit your museum and understand it is full of interesting items and lore."

It appeared we were the only visitors this morning. Mac told us to follow him and led us to our first stop, a suit of heavy armor from the twelfth century. Mr. Mac explained heavy armor such as this was more suitable for jousting in tournament events than for actual battle.

The armor was in great condition except for a few dents, which Mac told us were sustained by knights during actual jousts. He showed us some dark stains on the preserved leather trappings which he said were blood stains. I looked at Ken and said, "OK!"

Next we came to a huge broadsword which Mac told us had been used by Robert the Bruce during the battle with the English at Stirling Bridge in 1297. It was in perfect condition attesting to it's durability. Ken and I both reached up and touched the blade, rather a chilling experience. Further on we came to an English longbow and a quiver full of arrows. This lethal piece of military weaponry was used by the English archers with brutal effect against the Scots. Mac narrated a good English archer could launch up to twenty arrows a minute. Then added, but of course he could not sustain that rate of fire for long as he'd either run out of arrows, or strength, whichever came first.

On the opposite wall hung a huge tapestry from the thirteenth century. Mac narrated it was very typical of tapestries from the thirteenth century, depicting the hunt, the feast, and the drinking of spirits. I looked at Ken and he said, "Looks like fun to me." I nodded my agreement saying I think we would have enjoyed the revelry. The tapestry was beautiful and looked as though it could have been made only a few years ago rather than eight hundred, a real testament to the to the quality of the material and workmanship.

There were also old manuscripts, lists of names, miscellaneous writing pens, dishes and household furniture, all from the period 1200-1800. Mac's museum was very impressive. Completing our tour we thanked him and left a nice contribution in the "Help Maintain" box. With Mac's permission we took a couple photos and left.

****

We next walked across town to the old Church of Scotland which had been rebuilt in 1709, much of the original church having been destroyed by fire in 1678. We noticed that some of the pews, the altar, and a few icons dated back to the earlier time. Everything was beautifully maintained and their appearance caused us both to experience an unusual feeling. It was easy to sense God had spent a lot of his time here over the centuries, and we were somehow encroaching on an era long past.

Reverend Paul Seymour greeted us in his clerical robes which were another page out of that previous era. He stood, five-foot-ten, erect, 170 pounds, blonde hair, blue eyes, and projected an aura of confidence and piety. He did nothing to change our view that the Penoaken folk had a special aura about them. Everything here bespoke of antiquity and tradition.

We asked the good Reverend if we might begin by touring the old church cemetery and he quickly agreed. As we went outside and entered the sacred grounds, we marveled at how well maintained everything was.

Even the old headstones from centuries gone by were still readable, October 10, 1178, July 7, 1310, May 30, 1545, and so on. The latest date we noted was November 11, 2006, a child named Mary Craig, age 6 months.

After we concluded our walk through the cemetery, Reverend Seymour took us to the church library of records. Here stacked on shelves and in bookcases were volumes of somewhat dusty ledgers, and lists of transactions of all kinds dating from 1709.

Being interested in Scottish lore and history, we asked permission to peruse some of the old journals? I had selected four years at random, 1715, 1725, 1740, and 1755. I had no particular reason to pick these dates, but reasoned they would consume more than the time I had available. Looking through the journals would be cursory at best. The good Reverend offered to be at our beckon to answer any questions. I thought, *Gadzooks, what more could we ask for?* Within the next few minutes he laid the four annual records before us. We were to learn the church's annual ledgers were actually capsulated summations of important events or occurrences which took place within it's jurisdiction during each year, sort of a mini-history.

I suggested to Ken, "We'll each take two of the journals and if you find something of interest let me know." I selected 1725 and 1755 and Ken took the others. We put on surgical gloves, both were excited about this venture, and our tedious task began. It was probable we would not complete our effort today; thus, I asked the Reverend for permission to return in the morning. He quickly agreed.

At about three o'clock, after more than three hours of searching, I stumbled on an entry in the journal dated 1755 that, like a thunderbolt, grabbed my attention…. *An excited hunter* reported to the good Reverend Paul, the minister of the church at that time…*that he found the village of Auralee missing*. Gone. Nothing remained where it used to be. Narry man, nor beast could be found; further interrogation by Reverend Paul seemed to substantiate the hunter's story.

I could not comprehend the meaning of the hunter's claim, and thought it best to study the contents of this incredible report in the morning. Reverend Seymour had already given us permission to return. Ken and I left and returned to the Inn. On the way I told Ken of finding something in the 1755 register worth following up on and would explain later. That evening we enjoyed a couple of IPA ales, discussed our upcoming training for the hunt, and enjoyed dinner. Before turning in I again mentioned my discovery at the church to Ken, but didn't have anything specific to tell him. Ken said, "Well, looks as though we have another ghost story forthcoming."

On the morning of May 13th we hurried through breakfast and returned to the church at nine o'clock, anxious to restart our investigation of the report I had found in the 1755 ledger. I told Reverend Seymour I would later need his help, and he replied, "Fine."

Ken and I rushed to the viewing table and using surgical gloves I carefully reopened the 1755 ledger to the page which contained my "discovery." The entry was clearly noted May 20, 1755 and was reported and signed by a respected local hunter, one Haggis Frisbee as follows:

I be walken in the dales about 20 km north and west of Penoaken intending to visit thee wee village o' Auralee, but I see it nawas there. The bridge 'cross the cree begone, so I wadded 'cross the cree as the water be lower than usual. I find na path, na village, na people, na houses, na tools, and na animals. It be deathly still... na sound, na wind, na footprints. I be either lost or gone daffy. I be 'fraid the devil be here so I ran back 'cross thee cree and come to ye.

We hurried through the remaining pages of the ledger but could find no further mention of this incredible account. I thought, *Perhaps it was only the hunter's dream, or if it was ever substantiated by the church, perhaps it was considered too fearful to let it spread and time finally eroded any memory of Auralee's disappearance.*

I checked the death register for Haggis Frisbee…. *He died on May 21, 1755, the day following his "discovery"* and was buried in the church cemetery. No reason for death was given, perhaps from fright? I had to ask Reverend Seymour about this entry and reasoned that if there was any credence to the story, he would know of it.

When I brought this up to Reverend Seymour, he opened the journal to the page I had indicated…. *The page was empty…* there was no account by a person named Haggis Frisbee… nothing. I was totally flabbergasted and didn't know how to act. I flipped quickly back and forth through the pages to no avail… *there was nothing.* There was no use making an excuse, it could only dig my hole deeper. Eventually I replied, "Sir, please accept my apologies, obviously I have made a mistake or perhaps am just dreaming."

The good Reverend looked quizzically at me saying, "That be alright, laddy. Sometimes even I feel these old records harbor strange messages we canna always understand." I replied, "Seems so. Anyway it will make a hell of a tale to tell." I quickly apologized for my demonic reference and Reverend Seymour smiled politely and just chuckled.

However, I wasn't going to forget what I had seen. As we left the church we walked through the cemetery to the area noted on the list where Haggis Frisbee was buried. There it was…barely readable, but with a piece of paper and a pencil I brushed across the inscription…*Haggis Frisbee, borne 11 March, 1720, died 21 May, 1755, he be a goode mann.* Now what? Perhaps I best let it go with the assumption my imagination got the best of me and I had read a dead man's story of an event evidently long forgotten by time.

However, I could not forget what I knew I had seen in the ledger. After lunch when we arrived for our hunting lesson at 2:00 PM, I said, "Henry, before we start I have a question. Ever hear of a old village around these parts called Auralee?" Henry studied for a moment and told us he had not. I continued, "How about a hunter from long ago named Haggis Frisbee?" Again he answered in the negative, but said, "Why do you ask?" I replied, "Oh, it's nothing of any importance, thanks."

****

Today was cloudy, a little cool, with an expected high of about 55F, but tomorrow sounded better, high of about 65F with bright sunshine. We hoped the forecasts here were better than they usually were in Chicago. Henry introduced us to our weapons for the hunt, two six shot, twelve gauge Winchesters.

He reviewed the procedures for loading, unloading, locking, and firing. After we practiced the procedures a few times, Henry opened a map on a nearby table and told us he would go over the route we should follow along with some other guidelines.

We were to drive north via a one lane dirt road (more like a path) some 10 km (6 miles) where we would intersect another lane near a large oak tree on our left (west). Drive about 6 km (3 ½ miles) and park at a small meadow where the path ends. From there we would pick our way northwest through fields of heather and forested areas for about 2 km (1¼) mile where we would begin to encounter meadows covered with mid-calf length prairie grass. Perfect habitats for grouse.

Henry explained that we should position ourselves, each at opposite ends of the meadow so that one could walk the field towards the other. When the grouse were raised, be certain to not fire toward your partner as we would be firing bird shot and it has a wide field of shot spread. Henry next provided us with compasses and two small flashlights. Then told us should we become lost, do not try to find our way out at night. He instructed us to sit it out until daybreak; then, if all else failed take a course southeast and eventually we'd find civilization. He emphasized, "This I tell ye for certain. ye need a medium weight sweater, rain poncho, hunting cap, some water, and food for two days."

We were confident we would be able to find our way and thanked Henry for his concerns. Henry added a hearty breakfast would await us at four o'clock. I said, "Golly, thanks, Henry, we couldn't ask for more." He smiled, "Ye be welcome, lads, ye now be ready to be a part o' old Scotland, good hunting."

It would soon be bedtime, but first things first, a light dinner and some Maclay's India Pale in *The Pub* was in order. We went to *The Pub* where I said to Ken, "What a day this has been. I am still befuddled over finding that record of a village's disappearance in 1755, and then having the record just vanish. Doesn't make any sense to me. Something very strange going on here. I know there has to be an answer. Sometime, maybe during the night, it will come to me." He answered, "Fred, as sure as my name is Ken Effington, I'll wager a guess that before we leave for home we will have the mystery solved."

CHAPTER 4

THE GROUSE HUNT

AY 14TH, the day of our great expedition, began early. As we awoke the stars were shinning brightly heralding the arrival of the fine day we had anticipated. It was still nighttime but the moon was so bright one could almost read by it. We quickly dressed and hurried off to breakfast. Not surprisingly, we would be dining alone. Only the chef was present. Shortly he delivered to us a magnificently prepared feast: good hot stout Scottish coffee with warm cream, hardy blueberry pancakes with assorted jams and syrups, scrambled eggs, lamb chops, and plenty of cold orange juice. Even a jigger of Scotch whisky was available for our coffee, which we declined.

At 4:30 Ken and I were at our starting point and Henry was waiting to greet us. "Mornen to ye, Fred and Ken," he said with a smile. "It be a magnificent day for hunting, and dona forget to carry ye backpacks at all times." We thanked him, rechecked our vehicle to make certain we had packed everything, got in, waved goodbye, and departed. We were not anticipating anything more exceptional than a pleasant day of bird hunting.

Ken was driving as we headed north on the narrow dirt road. He commented it looked as if we really had departed civilization and I chuckled, "Yep, guess we have at that." I looked around and we were really out in the country, nothing in sight but sky, a few white clouds, trees, our narrow dirt road, meadows (glens), clear air, and open space. I took a deep breath and then another, so exhilarating. It was 5:10 and the sun was only now beginning to rise. We were on our way for our great grouse shoot-out; the primary reason we were here and had been anticipating for the past two months.

As our path northward continued to narrow and become rougher, our progress was limited to a maximum of 15 km (9 mph). We realized Henry knew what he was talking about when he told us we would be venturing into an uninhabited area seldom visited by people, but was abundant with wildlife. It was a pristine place; seemed really not of this time.

It was a real change from what we were accustomed. When I took a deep breath there were no odors, only fresh crisp air. I remarked to Ken I didn't realize there was this much fresh air in the whole world.

Following our locally prepared map, a meadow appeared where our vehicle was to be parked. At this point the road ended and from now on we would hoof it. It was time to ready our gear and recheck our shotguns and packs. Everything appeared in order and we certainly didn't want to leave anything behind. After locking the car I said to Ken, "OK, *Stanley*, I'll take the far end on the first meadow and you push them through to me." He responded, "Right on, *Livingston*, let's go get dinner."

It was now 7:00 AM. Our first meadow was about a half mile long and 150 yards wide. As Ken walked toward me, he soon flushed a covey of grouse. As they took flight they were closest to Ken and a distance from me; he cut loose with a salvo. Boom! Boom! Two birds fell, spiraling to earth like a couple of planes shot from the sky. I commented to myself, *Can this be that easy?* I rushed to pick up our first kill, beautiful little birds; my reaction was one of sorrow that we had done this. But as Ken excitedly arrived to inspect his first victory, I recovered from my initial feelings and commented, "Well, buddy, three more and you will be an ace." As he stuffed the birds in his catch bag he grinned, "OK, the race is on."

We moved on through a forested area until we came to another, larger, meadow that was perhaps a mile in length and a couple hundred yards in width. It was my turn to walk the walk. Ken headed toward the far end of the meadow, stopping about half way, gave me a wave, and I moved toward him. It took me most of a hour to complete my journey and if there was any game around they were able to elude me in this large area. When arriving I said to Ken, "Well, that wasn't much fun was it?" He replied, "We will get them next time."

It was now almost ten o'clock; thus, we decided it was time to break for some lunch. We found a pleasant shady area at the far end of the meadow. It looked like a good place to sit and relax. We each took a good drink of water, removed from our knapsacks an apple, half of a roast beef sandwich, a small can of baked beans, and slowly devoured the feast. Actually it tasted good. We were hungry after all of our exercise. It was so pleasant here. The surrounding hills covered with heather in full bloom appeared as if they were covered with snow. The air was still except for the chattering and tweeting of a few birds; the sun peeked randomly through the branches of the trees as though it was playing hide-and-seek with us.

"Ken," I marveled, "where's the smog, the congestion, and the noise? It's almost as if this is another world." He grunted, "Hell, don't remind me. *Maybe we're lost in time for all I know and care.*" For just a moment Ken's comments stopped me. Had he considered how prophetic his comments seemed to me? Obviously, still influenced by my recent experience at the church, I just laughed and replied, "It'll never be the same when we return to ole Chicago, will it?"

At 10:45 we moved on through another larger forested area. Everything was becoming one-of-the-same. There were no longer any paths or indicators to help; thus, we needed to rely on our compasses to tell us in what direction we were going. Occasionally we both made notations of our readings as eventually we would need to backtrack on them. Definable landmarks were few, a hill here, a large crooked tree there. The forest was relatively thick; thus, not much sunshine found it's way to us and that made directional orientation spotty.

At 12:15 PM we came to another open area, about a half mile long an a half mile wide. It was Ken's turn again to walk the meadow, and would you believe it, he flushed another covey. Boom! Boom! Another bird headed for the ground! The remaining flock headed straight for me. Now it was my turn. Boom! Boom! Boom! Two more birds plummeted from the sky.

We collected our kill bringing our total to five birds. We commented this would be an adequate number for a good dinner when we returned to the Inn at Penoaken. We stood for a moment congratulating ourselves before I said, "Ken, it's now 1:00 PM and we should begin our trip back to our vehicle." Ken agreed. By now we were hungry again so we had another drink of water, some cheese, a slice of thick bread, another apple, and the last of our coffee. At 1:30 we packed up our knapsacks and headed back to Penoaken.

****

Almost immediately upon reentering the forest on our return trip to our vehicle, we began to feel disoriented. Initially everything seemed to look familiar, yet the further we went it really didn't. We continued to rely on our compasses which indicated the direction we believed we should go, but after about an hour, I said to Ken, "I think we have passed this place before." A large tree which bent at an awkward angle arose before us and both of us agreed we had been here before…apparently walking in a circle. It was now 2:30 and we needed to get our bearings established fast. After checking my compass which seemed OK, I said, "We must be going in the right direction, let's continue."

Forty-five minutes later we arrived back at the same place, the large, oddly bent tree. I turned to Ken and said, "What the deuce is happening here? How can we be walking in a circle? I think we're lost!" Ken responded, "Yep, Fred, I believe we are, but how do you figure this could happen?" I simply said, "Ken, I don't know or understand any of this."

We tried to locate the sun, but because of the density of the foliage and with the day becoming overcast, we could not see it. I said to Ken, "We should continue for another hour and if we are still undecided about where we are, we must find a place to spend the night, and begin anew in the morning." He agreed and we moved on. At four fifteen it was getting dark and it did not appear we were making any headway. Obviously it was time to set up "camp" for the night.

Nearby was a large oak tree whose trunk provided room for each of us to rest our backs against; the ground was level, not rocky, and it was covered with a cushion of thick low grass. We spread one poncho to be used as a ground sheet and put on our sweaters and hunting jackets. Our second poncho would be used as a cover to ward off any mist or early morning dew. Nighttime temperatures would hover around 25C (45F). Cool, but the trees would ward off wind, and light rain. At four forty-five we ate our last meal of the day: bread, cheese and cold cuts.

Near our "home" for the evening was a large stump upon which we could sit while discussing our dilemma. Neither of us were afraid, but by the same token we were concerned about our situation. I said to Ken, "What we have here is not just a piece of Scottish lore, it is real." He replied, "Don't know, ole friend, what we have here, just don't know."

It was now dark and very still. We heard only an owl hooting a love call into the vastness of the night, and a squawky bird that sounded like a monkey, perhaps a grackle. No other sounds penetrated the density of this night's darkness.

It was as if our world had vanished and left us here alone in a world of stark nothingness. At 7:00 we retired hoping to get some sleep before renewing our efforts in the morning. We estimated that first light might penetrate our world at around 5:30 to 6:00 AM.

We decided to take Henry's advise and in the morning set our course to the southeast in the hope of finding anything resembling civilization. We leaned against our tree, covered ourselves with our second poncho, and told each other goodnight. Fortunately we both fell asleep, not a sound sleep, but at least it was rest.

****

At about 12:45 AM on the morning of May 15th something jarred my senses. I awoke and listened…. It sounded like water rippling over rocks as in rapids! Funny! *There wasn't any water around here before!* Yes, it was definitely the sound of water. I shook Ken who awoke with a, "Huh!" "Ken, listen…do you hear water running?" He yawned, stared into the night and answered, "Yes, Fred, it does sound like water running. Where is it coming from?" I responded, "Don't know, it wasn't here last evening." We both arose, put on our ponchos, and began to look around. We used our small flashlights, directing the beams back and forth to our front and to each side.

The first thing we noticed was a path running in an westerly direction, which wasn't there before. I said, "Come on, this definitely means something. Let's see where this path goes." We moved cautiously to the west, in the direction of the water sound. Shortly we came to a curve in the path, directed our flashlights, and rounded the corner. We could verily make out a large object ahead of us in the distance, a stone structure of some sort!

Coming closer we could see that it was a bridge, a stone bridge crossing over a wide stream with rapids running beneath it. These things were not here last night. Ken spoke in rather an alarmed voice, "Fred, what in Christ's name is going on? I don't think we are dreaming, are we?" I answered, "No, we are not dreaming and I don't know what the hell is going on."

For an instant a recurring thought flashed across my mind, *The church record…Auralee's disappearance…1755?* The thought soon vanished.

I said, "Ken, come on let's cross the bridge!" He chokingly whispered, "Yes, what else can we do? Let's collect our things and go for it." We grabbed our packs. I continued, "Perhaps from here to oblivion, but here we go." The time was 2:00 AM on May 15, 2008…*or so we thought.* My last observation before we left was, "Ken, remember this stump. It could be useful to us as a future landmark."

CHAPTER 5

A PLACE CALLED AURALEE

W E MOVED cautiously across the stone bridge; though it was still dark, we could see our path continued straight ahead, then disappeared beyond a grove of tall trees. We slowly continued walking. It was very still and at first we did not see nor hear anything unusual; it was scary and caused us to wonder again where we were. Then we heard the sound of a bird singing and in the distance *a cow was mooing*! Yes, we were certain of it and the sounds continued to repeat themselves. This area was supposedly uninhabited, but the cow mooing was defiantly a sound of civilization nearby! Excited now, we continued walking.

We inched our way forward; at a clump of trees the path curved to our left and as we turned the corner the area became much more open and the night was moon bright. I said to Ken, "Let's find a place to sit and wait until dawn before going on." He agreed and at the side of the path was another indication of civilization, a rustic wooden fence.

We found a place on it which sufficed for a bench and parked ourselves. As he sat down Ken remarked, "What have we here, ole sage?" "Beats me," I replied, "guess we'll find out in time."

We broke out an apple, took a swig of water, and just leaned back. *I thought once again about the entry in the church journal which subsequently wasn't there.* That experience will just not go away… is it possible we are lost…somewhere in time?

For the next few hours it remained dark; we rested and pondered on our presence in this place. I was anxious to continue on; at 5:00 AM the glow of the sun started to illuminate the eastern sky behind us. It was a very welcome sight. Ken yawned, and I said, "Come on, sleepyhead. Excitement may be lurking just around the corner."

****

Bravely and with a sense of confidence we stepped into a blossoming morning on our trek to…we hoped civilization. As the darkness faded into day, in the distance we began to see structures!

I looked at Ken and muttered, "Houses, look, Ken, houses." It was our first sign of hope that we were actually approaching someplace inhabited by humans. "See the smoke rising from their chimneys. It's a village, Ken, come on." He answered, "Good God, Fred, you're right, but where are we?" I said, "Who cares? It's a very welcome sight, let's hope we will be welcome."

Cautiously we shuffled forward. There were lights coming from some of the houses, and a dog barked wistfully somewhere in the distance. It was obvious we were approaching a village, but what village? There was nothing indicated on our map? I thought, *If this is for real, it certainly is not in our nominal game plan.* We moved closer until the houses appeared more clearly. They were constructed of stone and had thatched roofs…*as they would have been built 200 or more years ago.*

****

Quite suddenly a portly gentleman neatly dressed in eighteenth century attire, perhaps forty-five years old, 5'9" tall, 175 pounds, graying hair, his beard clipped short, stepped from the doorway of the house nearest us. Then just as suddenly another similarly dressed man appeared from around the corner of the house and joined him. We clearly saw them shake hands, and the portly one was smoking a long stemmed pipe; the smoke curling upwards with every puff.

Ken and I stood transfixed. We were now in plain sight; when they saw us they quickly turned and stared intently. I quietly said, "Come on, Ken, let's see what we have here," and the two of us began walking slowly toward them. They continued to stand like statues and stare; we must have looked odd in our twenty-first century attire and on top of that, we carried weapons. As we neared, they slowly began to move away from us. I said, as pleasantly as I could, "Hello, my name is Fred Mitchell and this is Ken Effington. We are from America, across the ocean and a long way from home. What village might this be?"

A long silence prevailed until the portly gentleman replied, "Sirs, I be Angus Macgregor and this be our respected Mayor, Mister Robert Bright. Gentlemen ye be in the village of Auralee in Scotland and 'tis the year of our Lord, 1757... America...ye say ye be from? That be a colony o' England?" I answered, "Yes, Sir, that is correct." *I realized he must be speaking from a point of view that was prior to the Revolutionary War.* Angus Macgregor continued, "We nay be expecting visitors, from beyond the ocean, even though this be thee 15th of May." We didn't know what the 15th of May had to do with anything, but supposed we would find out sooner or later.

But the year 1757 grabbed me...*Could this be the village I saw referred to in the church historical register which was reported missing by the hunter, Haggis Frisbee, a day prior to his untimely death. The same report which had mysteriously disappeared from the church record as I tried to show it to the reverend?*

I whispered, "Ken, what have we here?" He looked at me quizzically saying, "I have no idea." For a moment we rigidly stood, mesmerized by what we had just heard. Finally I asked, "1757, you said?" Angus continued, "Aye, laddy, why be ye so surprised?"

After some thought I slowly and deliberately dispensed my reply. "Well, Sirs, you see…we come here from the year 2008…which is 251 years…from the date you just gave us." Personally I knew they would think that impossible. But to our surprise, Angus calmly answered, "I see, gentlemen. Ye ha' come a long way, be ye lost?" I agreed we were either lost or quite possibly only dreaming.

Angus, turned to Mr. Bright and after a short conference replied, "Laddy, nay, Freddy, this nay be a dream and, yes, there be an explanation but as yet ye canna expect to understand it.

"Later we shall take ye to visit the Elder, Reverend Dundee, who can best explain thee predicament, and perhaps also your presence among us here. But first we let you see our village. This day be a festival day. We call it the Festival of Life and festivals occur once every three months and this be the Great Festival which happens only once each year on the 15th o' each May. Perhaps in time it will come to have greater importance to ye."

Angus said, "Come wi' me, lads, and be ye o' good fortune and spirit. Mr. Bright goes to inform the Reverend Dundee o' ye comen. Now I tak' ye to see our village." To say the least we were somewhat shaken. We hadn't yet been able to confront what was happening to us and the only thing we could do now was to follow along and just let things happen, so like good soldiers we said, "Yes, Sir," and started off with him.

As we began our trek we paid close attention to the details of our surroundings. I turned to Ken and said, "Can you believe where we are? It has to be the village referred to in the church records." Ken sputtered, "Fred, I don't think this is real. It is only a dream, and soon we are going to wake up." My reply was, "Too early to tell yet, but I venture we are heading into an exciting experience."

The village appeared neat, clean, and orderly. Everything and everyone definitely looked of eighteenth century origin. Many streets were paved with stone, the houses were of stone masonry with thatched roofs, smoke curled from every chimney, flower beds and flower boxes were everywhere, most houses had storage sheds for their horses, and most homes seemed to have water pumps and outhouses. There were lots of trees; some had children's swings dangling from their branches.

Arriving at the festival we noted the women were dressed in colorful long dresses and bonnets of the period. The men's attire was a mixture. Some wore red, blue, and black plaid kilts, some appeared to be in their daily work clothes, and a few looked to be dressed in their Sunday best. Several people were hurrying toward the festival carrying large baskets of food and other items with which to stock the booths. When we rounded the corner we entered a large plaza whose dimensions were well over a large city block. In the center was a large water fountain which we were informed supplied a good portion of Auralee's drinking water. Water for laundry and bathing came primarily from cisterns filled by abundant rainfall. The children were laughing, screaming, and playing a game similar to the game we call Tag. Everyone seemed quite happy.

I implored, "Mr. Macgregor, Sir, we are still so very, very confused, being here in a place which is obviously not of our time. We are anxious to meet Reverend Dundee and hope he has some explanations for us." He smiled, a very jolly smile. Standing in front of us wearing his tartan in full regalia, I couldn't help but like him. He provided a comforting image of trust for which we were grateful. He said, "Freddy, me lad, again I say, do ye nay fret. All answers will come ye way soon. In the meantime you have places still to visit and people yet to meet."

****

Just beyond the square Angus led us to his home. He said, "Lads, I want ye to meet my two daughters, Jean, 21 years and Mary, 17 years." It was a rather large house and I expected it to hold a rather large family. We entered, looked about, and were surprised to see how pleasant and spacious the interior was. There were several large quilted chairs, plus a large dining room table with six ladder back chairs. The kitchen was separated from the living room by a serving counter, much like our twenty-first century houses were arranged. Angus quickly added his wife had passed on a couple years ago and added, "The will o' God be final."

Angus continued, "Now I want ye to meet Jean and Mary. Please ye sit here, and I will fetch them." We sat down and Ken questioned me, "Fred, for Pete's sake, how do we get out of this place?"

I responded, "Ken, please relax. It appears our questions need to be deferred until we see Reverend Dundee. We came to Scotland for a change of pace, and I guess that is what we are getting, OK, ole buddy?" He stammered a weak affirmative response, "Yeh, I guess we are…in spades." He went on with his spiel, "But I am still more than a little concerned." I snarled, "Ken, please cut this harangue out. I won't listen to you anymore until we see Reverend Dundee. Stop now, finis, alto, halt your panic right here!" Finally he seemed to come around, smiled and said, "OK, partner, you are probably right. I'll be good from now on, I promise." I looked at Ken, winked, smiled and said, "Nuff said, ole buddy."

****

Shortly when Angus returned he was followed closely by his two daughters. I was startled, no *stunned,* at their appearance! They were both beautiful, and I do mean beautiful young ladies. Raven hair covered their shoulders, their flashing Scottish blue eyes momentarily mesmerized me, and their peaches and crème complexions were purely perfection. They seemed to glide across the floor like two slim perfectly matched bookends. They almost looked like twins, except one was an inch or so taller.

I was thunderstruck and my heart skipped several beats. I had not expected this would have been possible in 1757, but here they were. I reasoned, well, why not? I am going to stop taking anything for granted. Angus said, "Freddy, Kenny, lads, this be my daughter, Jean." She curtsied daintily. "And this be my younger daughter, Mary, who is planned to wed in June." She also curtsied.

I stuttered, "Angus we are humbled in the presence of such beauty. Your daughters are like two lovely roses reaching out to greet the splendid first rays of the morning sun." The girls giggled and seemed to blush a little. Angus answered, "Thank ye, lads, for ye graciousness." I thought, *Beats the hell out of anything our country club, including Samantha, has to offer.* I could see Ken was in absolute agreement. His mouth was slightly askew and he smiled.

Angus continued, "Freddy, Kenny, lads, the girls want to take ye on a tour of our wee village. When ye return I willa meet thee in the square for a bit o' food before we go to meet Reverend Dundee." Ken and I couldn't agree fast enough, we were both quickly approaching a state beyond our initial shock, and we were definitely hungry. We left the house with the girls. They seemed giddy in their delight. I was so taken by Jean's natural beauty and demeanor that I was lost for anything to say. She walked beside me like a well choreographed dancer, so smooth, so graceful. I looked at Ken as if to say, *come on, can this be really happening?*

Jean finally spoke, "Freddy, I hope ye like our wee village and I wish ye to be stayen wi' us for a long time." I didn't yet understand her implications so I only smiled and said, "Thank you, Jean. We will see." We walked past the village church and next to it was an attached building which served as a school. Jean was quick to tell us it was run by mothers who contributed whatever they could to help the children learn a wee bit o' reading and writing. Apparently no formalized curriculum existed. We walked down several streets. The homes were all neat and amply gardened. Even the areas where their stock was kept appeared orderly, clean, and we noticed no odors.

We returned to the festival where we again saw the large fountain in the center of the square with several water spigots sticking out from it. Elsewhere around the square were tents and many tables covered with food. In abundance were meat pies, roasted lamb, sausages, various wild game, and dishes containing several kinds of vegetables were steaming over hot coals of peat moss and pine wood. For the children's delight there was candy on a stick, and several tents housed special entertainment such as juggling and storytelling for audiences of all ages.

At last, to Ken's pleasure, there appeared a giant wooden keg dispensing heather ale. His face lit up like he had just found a long lost friend. Scottish pipers, drummers, fifers, were accompanying dancing and controlled merriment. We were impressed. Everything was orderly, entertaining, and everyone seemed to be having fun.

Several adult games were in process: horseshoe pitching, lawn bowling, and races. It was explained the people from the Glen of Auralee's other two small communities of Nevis and Dee were in attendance and friendly competition was in order. Another comment was offered which was not clear. *We were in the Village of Auralee, and now a reference to a Glen of Auralee?* Moving on, in some tents, storytellers entertained their audiences, young and old, with strange fascinating mystic tales. I thought this was an area in which Ken and I might excel.

Ken excused himself saying he was thirsty and would like to stop for an ale. Mary was quick to say she would accompany him in case he be in need of help. I thought, *Not for the ale drinking, but perhaps for something else.* Jean and I sat on a bench. Though impressed with the goings-on, I wanted to talk with her. I found myself becoming attached to her already and asked, "Jean, what is it you do everyday to keep yourself busy, and are you happy?"

She was spontaneous with her response. "Aye, Freddy, I be very happy and ne'er have any desire to leave, but I be waiten for these years for someone to share this life wi' me...and might ye be the one sent to me?" *I had no idea of what she meant but I would delay my asking for awhile in hopes she or Reverend Dundee might clear it up for me.*

"To keep busy, that be easy. I care for our home, help prepare the meals, secure food and water, do other household duties, help at the school one day each week, go to church on Sunday, join in festival activities, and other special activities that take place, attend quilten bees, and read every book I can find. Unfortunately we ha' only a limited number of them, so I just read them again. I love dancen and singen at the festival. And there are my friends, the wee birds and animals. I have names for all o' them. I be happy, Freddy, but it will please me greatly if you will stay here wi' us...of course, if that be possible." Finally, I asked, "What do you mean, if that be possible?" Jean smiled sweetly, "Perhaps ye willa find out when we visit wi' Reverend Dundee."

****

We returned to the festival area; Angus, Ken, and Mary joined us. It was "cafeteria" style. We took a wooden plate, knife, and spoon, went from table-to-table, and selected our foods.

Passing by the ale keg, we men each drew a pint and took a swig. Ken looked at me and said, "Hey, ole buddy, it's different but think I could get used to it in time." I thought, *Yeh, in about two minutes.* The girls took water from the fountain. We sat at a table nearby and ate. There were no napkins so we had to just be neat and careful, or wipe our hands on our clothing. The girls had handkerchiefs. Small talk followed, with Angus asking us what we thought of Auralee so far.

Ken said, "Fine, Sir, just fine." I expanded a bit, "Angus, so far we are very impressed with your Auralee, but we are yet so full of unanswered questions and are very anxious to meet Reverend Dundee. I hope you understand." Angus answered, "Aye, Freddy, and it now be time. Let us go to see Reverend Dundee, the Elder." It was now noon.

I said, "Angus, before we go may I take a short walk with Jean. I want to get to know her better and he responded, "Aye, laddy, we will meet ye here at one o'clock." I told him thanks and we left. Ken went to revisit the heather bar, and Mary said she was going to meet her promised.

Jean and I walked north out of the village past a small wooded area. The day was warm and pleasant, the countryside fresh and invigorating. It seemed as though I had returned to my childhood just a few years past.

I stopped and looked at Jean, bonnie Jean, and said, "Earlier you mentioned that you hoped I would stay as though you had been expecting me. What did you mean?" Jean looked me straight in the eyes. God, she looked so innocent, so pure of heart, so beautiful, I just melted. For a short while she did not speak.... But then, "Oh, Freddy, I hope ye na think me bold, but I nay have found a lad in Auralee that I feel I can marry and spend my life devoted to. A few years ago I had a dream and it told me to be patient for someday a lad will come to Auralee who you will love. Since I first saw you I have had a special feelen that ye be that person." She looked so tender, so afraid, as if she may have shocked me.

I took her by the arm and pulled her close to me. "Jean, dear Jean, I am so glad you told me of this. You see, I too have had a strange feeling. A feeling like I have known you before, and could love you dearly. But, Jean, I don't know if I could remain in Auralee forever. Our lives are so separated by time, our cultures so different. I guess we need to see what Reverend Dundee can tell us." I took her by the hand and said, "Let's go," and we walked slowly back to the fountain to meet Angus. He was waiting with Ken and said, "Follow me, lads, for Reverend Dundee be expecting us."

Farmer's Croft and his Faithful Companions

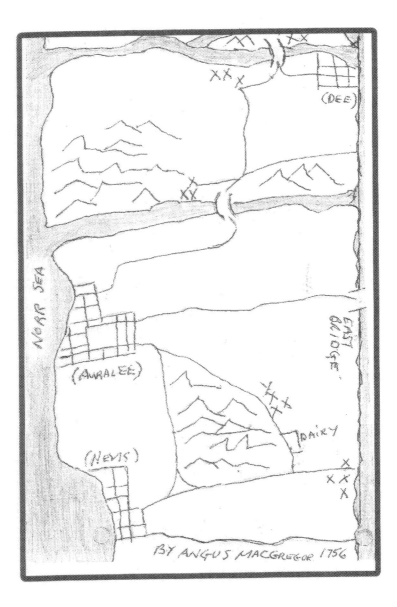

BY ANGUS MACGREGOR 1756

View of Auralee Looking North from Pasture

WILD MEADOW FLOWERS

CHAPTER 6

VISIT WITH REVEREND DUNDEE

W<small>E WALKED</small> just beyond the southern boundary of Auralee to the home of a man referred to as *The Elder...* for in him was invested the understanding of Glen Auralee's deliverance into a life eternal.

We arrived and The Elder, Reverend Dundee, was sitting on his porch; several wooden chairs surrounded him. He looked in every way a senior Scotsman, some 50 or so years of age, five-foot-ten, red hair and beard with a sprinkling of gray. He was dressed in his finest kilt and a Scottish terrier sat by his side. He said, "Gentlemen, good afternoon to ye; please sit wi' me."

We selected a chair and sat down. Reverend Dundee continued, "Gentlemen, how canna be o' help to ye?" Angus took the ball. "Sir, Fred Mitchell and Kenny Effington arrived in Glen Auralee early this morning via the bridge, and as this be May 15th they were able to cross into our time. They be from the year o' our Lord 2008. I remind ye o' Jean's dream and believe she and Freddy already have an interest in each other. Thee lads ha' come wi' questions to ask ye." Reverend Dundee spoke in a firm but fatherly voice. "Aye, Freddy and Kenny, but first I will try to help ye understand what happened here in the year 1754. Just sit ye with an open mind and listen."

He began, "For many years before 1754 Scotland had been in turmoil fighting wars with England. Our wee Glen Auralee had removed itself from all that was broilen outside it. At that time our Elder be one, the Reverend Charles Toomley. He had led us to be responsive to all God's tenets, almost to a fault.

"One day in May 1754 Reverend Toomley went to the highest point in Glen Auralee and prayed for several days asking God's deliverance from all the frailties of outside lands. When he returned after two days he told us God had delivered to him a heavenly ultimatum:

" *'At midnight of this day, May 14th, 1754, Glen Auralee wi' all her folk and attachments will be delivered from commitment to the old world and it's tyme, into a land all it's own…for eternity. And from this day forward for each day passen Auralee tyme, five days shall pass in the old world.*

'Further, from this day forward na citizen of Glen Auralee be able to leave it's boundaries. To do so would forfeit his or her place in the House of God and their soul rendered to the regions of space beyond heaven to roam helplessly forever.

'Each year from midnight on May 14th, until midnight on May 15th, the door to Glen Auralee be open via the bridge across the Easterly Creek. Should someone venture into Auralee, they be welcomed, but must leave the Glen by midnight on the 15th or forever forfeit their opportunity to do so and be subject forever to all the tenets of Glen Auralee.

'Actions of wanton violence nay be tolerated and if condemned that person or persons shall be made to leave Auralee under the second tenet above.' "

Reverend Dundee paused. We were in awe at what we had been told…for each year that goes by in Auralee five zoom by outside it's boundary. *We noted that May 15th was the same day in both the years of 2008 and 1757!*

Reverend Dundee continued, "As for Reverend Toomley, when he finished his instructions to us, he just walked away toward the mountains and we nay ha' found any trace o' him. He now be residen with God, his price he paid to deliver the folk he loved so much from harm."

Ken commented, "Best we be out of here by midnight." Reverend Dundee looked at us and said, "Perhaps it be so, but before ye decide, do ye hav' any questions?"

I quickly replied, "Yes, Sir, I do, but may I have a little time to consider them in the light of what I have just heard?" Reverend Dundee answered, "Aye, o' course ye can, laddy, and I be here when ye be ready to ask me o' them." I said, "Thank you, Sir." Ken and I left to return to Angus's home and as we reached his house I explained to Angus and Jean that Ken and I needed some time alone before we returned to see Reverend Dundee. They both quickly understood and we left and walked to a small glen south of Angus's home.

****

On the way, Ken commented, "Good God, Fred, is this weird or what?" I retorted, "No, Ken, don't think anything we have seen or heard is weird; however, we best consider well our options for they are open to us for only a short time." Ken replied, "Yep, that's right, but what is there to consider? Would you really consider staying here forever?"

I answered, "Ken, never said I could stay here, even though it seems to offer peace, contentment, and happiness. How many of these things do we have in good ole 2008?" Ken said, "You got me there, pal, but how happy might you be scratching a living from the ground, planting a seed here and catching a fish there?

"Not me, ole friend, I'd miss my car, my TV, and my country club crowd." I retorted, "Damn it, Ken, think! think! You gotta know there is more to life than superficial things." I asked Ken to sit some distance away from me for the next few minutes so we both might think independently of each other. Ken agreed and the following minutes were the most difficult of my life. My mind raced back and forth like a carousel with my brain playing the old song, *My Merry-Go- Round Broke Down*.

Finally I said, "Ken, let's go." He slouched over and I could tell he was disturbed in anticipation of my decision. He said, "Well, ole buddy, what is it you have come up with?" I responded that he would know my decision soon and we began walking back toward Angus's home.

****

When we arrived he and Jean were awaiting us. As I had much to say to Jean, I asked Ken to return to the festival and wait for me there. He seemed quite pleased to accommodate my request and departed.

I took Jean by the hand and said, "Jean, please come walk with me. We have so much to talk about and so precious little time to do it before I must make my decision to either return to 2008 or to stay here forever. It will not be an easy decision for me." Jean smiled broadly, as she still retained at least a small bit of hope that I might stay here with her.

I said to myself, *There is no question about my fascination with this Scottish lass. But there are major hurdles which would have to be overcome, and I am not yet positive we could handle them, not the least of which, would we both stay happy together for eternity?*

As we walked south I watched the countryside with pastures full of cattle and sheep being herded very efficiently by Scottish sheep dogs. Shortly we came to a small clearing surrounded by mighty oak trees whose branches were full of little birds feverishly singing to us their cheerful songs. Jean said, "The wee wrens be me favorite, Freddy. They tell me I be aliven in a blessed place." I answered, "Yes, Jean and I am sure they are right."

We sat at a wooden table, built much like our picnic tables back home. Jean told me she often came to one of these places with the children from her school class to talk about nature, the flowers, the birds, the cattle, and how they all were placed here by God.

I thought, *Rather like a Biology class. How neat this is. How natural. I considered Samantha and how utterly the opposite of Jean she was. Sam, self centered, selfish of thought, and inconsiderate of others around her...and I had been in love with her?*

I pondered, *Could Jean leave Auralee with me?* The thought passed as suddenly as it arrived. Of course she could not leave, nor could she ever be happy if she did. She could never overcome the span of years that lay between our two cultures, and I wouldn't want her to try. I reconciled myself to the fact, the only way we could be together was for me stay here with her...forever.

But could I do it? I was not yet ready to answer that question. Time had slipped by, and I said, "Jean, let's go back." I put my arm about her shoulder and pulled her close to me; she was daintily responsive. After a couple minutes of walking, I said. "You are nervous, Jean, and I am so sorry to make you feel that way."

Jean responded, "Oh, Freddy, I do wish there be more time. I know ye must make your mind up soon and only wish ye to make the choice which be best for thee." I thought, *Gad's, what unselfishness this is, so pure of thought...*and I knew she truly meant it. I responded, "Jean, bonnie Jean, may I kiss you?" She stopped, looked up to me, and smiled in her lovely, dainty little way. "Oh, yes, Freddy, please do and know it be the kiss I be awaiten for all these years."

I took her in my arms, kissed her softly but passionately and said, "Thank you, Jean. With each moment that passes my feelings for you deepen." My mind was screaming with *should I stay, should I go?* There were no answers...only confusion flashed throughout my brain, like little flashes of psychogenic lights.

"Freddy, I be sure thee be sent to me and ha' been waiten for ye to come. I will be waiten thee forever, and always love ye dearly." Well that bottom lined it for Jean. For myself, there were doubts. I could forever dearly love and cherish this darling young lass. But my doubts ran along the lines of whether I could adjust to mid-eighteenth century living and be able to make Jean happy. At last I said, "Jean, please give me a little more time to consider my decision." She replied, "Aye, Freddy, I await ye decision wi' all the hope my heart has."

****

We continued to walk and Jean suggested we cut catty-cornered across a good sized pasture in order to save some time. The pasture was full of cattle and tended by a young man and his dog. As we crossed, he waved, and we waved back. She told me the young man's name be Theodore, a son of a nearby crofter (farmer), and his dog be named Lassie Girl. I guessed she really knew everybody. It was another pleasant rural scene where everything seemed to be in harmony.

Coming from the twenty-first century it was almost like the sound of silence. There were no honking cars, noisy copters, blaring sirens, no hurry-there-hurry-here...only contentment.... Wow!

****

I turned to Jean and said, "Living in such a small place as this, does it ever make you feel uncomfortable or confined?" She spontaneously replied, "Oh, no, Freddy, I be ne'er bored. There be much for me to do and also places to go and visit. You see besides Auralee we have two other wee villages of Nevis and Dee as well as several croft (farm) communities.

"There be the annual Festival o' Life to prepare for and attend each May 15th - it be our Deliverance Day. Then there are the summer, fall and winter festivals as well as our Christmas season which extends from December 23rd through January 2nd. I ha' my school children to teach one day each week, church to attend, there be quilten parties for we women, my daily housework, cleanen, cooken, menden and such. I read all I can get my hands on, and my favorite pastime is watchen and talken to the wee birds and animals.

"Ye see, Freddy, there be much for everyone to keep themselves well busy in Glen Auralee. It has now been over three years since our deliverance and no one has even suggested they would want it to be any different here.

"I shall pray for ye to stay, Freddy, but if ye nay stay, I will wait ye forever in the blessed hope ye one day will return to me."…. Brother, how I was hurting.

We reached Angus's house and I told him I needed to talk with Ken before meeting with him and Jean at Reverend Dundee's place. It would be about an hour. I left for the festival and found Ken in deep conversation with a cute, robust, blond lass by the name of Heather Crawford. Yep, that's right, Heather. Don't know where she came from, but she was a delightful representative of Scotland's female persuasion. It seemed to me Auralee was well supplied with lovely ladies.

Ken excused himself saying, "Heather, perhaps after we visit with Reverend Dundee, I shall be able to return. If I do and you still are here we can resume our discussion." She said, "Aye, Kenny, I be here." He smiled at her and we headed to the place where Jean and I had met a short while ago.

On the way I said, "Ken, dear old friend, we have some serious talking to do in a very short time. Are you ready?" Ken sensed my urgency and replied, "Hell, Fred, this scares me, but I can tell it's crunch time." I answered, "Yes, Ken, it is that in spades."

CHAPTER 7

THE DECISION

I said, "Ken…you know what? We're watching time go by like, here it is…there it goes. After we leave nothing will remain of this journey except our collective memories. We'll have fun someday telling our grandkids, if we have any, about this trip. Exciting thought, huh? Except we'll probably never tell them. They would never believe us, and why should they? I am not even sure I really do. However, one thing is for certain, the longer I am here in Auralee the more it becomes obvious to me how little we know about life and all it's permutations…like we have just stepped beyond the limits of our perceived understanding of life and time. How about you, Ken?"

He thought for a moment and replied, "Fred, you are getting philosophic and I'm having difficulty understanding your logic. Admittedly there have been some second thoughts about what has happened to us, but I can not justify chucking away life in 2008 for a small piece of 1757…. I am going home!"

I pondered my response and finally spoke…. "You are probably right, Ken. Back home we have budding careers, money in the bank, and a multitude of supposed friends. Yet here, along with ample peace and contentment, I have a girl waiting to love me forever…but there is always the consideration of whether I could really adjust to this time and be happy, or would she be happy with a man who has 2008 habits? A monumental dilemma awaits my answer. If appropriate answers are not forthcoming from Reverend Dundee that would change my decision…*then I too… must go home!*"

After taking a last look around at the peaceful and serene countryside, time was of the essence, and we departed the rest area. If I am to leave, there must be a way to tell her quickly. Nothing could be said which would make my job easy. For Jean it would be disappointment beyond imagination. Her hopes that had arrived so suddenly would just as suddenly be dashed. But I had to keep in mind, should my decision be to leave Auralee, it was made with both our best interests in mind.

We approached Reverend Dundee's house; Jean and her father awaited our arrival. As we arrived it was obvious Jean was restless and it was apparent she had been going through some bad times since Ken and I left to take our walk. My feeling was something like death warmed over, but nevertheless I had to go on.

I began, "Reverend Dundee, Sir, this has been an extremely difficult time for Ken and myself and we have two very important questions to ask of you: First, please define the difference between Village of Auralee and Glen or Land of Auralee. Second, and most important, Sir, *if we decide to leave Auralee is it possible that we could return?*"

Reverend Dundee sat down, removed his cap, scratched his head, studied his response for a few moments, and began. "Lads, to ye first and the easiest question:

"Glen or Land Auralee be a land area, by ye measurement, o' about 30 square miles. It be bounded to the west by a sheltered bay of the Norr Sea through which a warm southern current flows keep our temperatures warmer than they otherwise would be. To the east by the East Creek, to the north by munros (mountains) which protect we folk from the harsh winter winds, and to the south by steep ravines abundant wi' bramble brush.

"Withen the boundaries of Glen Auralee we ha' three villages, Auralee being the largest, Dee to the northeast, and Nevis on the sea to ye southwest. There be several crofter (farmer) associations spread about the land. This be a wee land but a blessed land."

Reverend Dundee's answer to our second question rather surprised us...."Aye, Freddy, *perhaps* one could return. If ye love someone enough then *perhaps* it could be possible; but if there be a chance, the next opportunity would be a year from today by our time, next May 14th at midnight. And mind ye, Freddy and Kenny, I canna say that any other time it be possible. It is only me thinken. I canna speak for the Lord." His answer surprised me, but thought, *At least the door is left ever so slightly open.*

It was now crunch time. I turned to Jean and struggled with my words, "Jean, in this very short time I have fallen very much in love with you, and believe you love me in return. That is what makes my words to you so difficult for me to say. Jean, I am not sure I could forsake my world of 2008 and be happy here, and if not, then your life would not be a good life either. I can find no answer to this dilemma. *Therefore, Ken and I have opted to leave Auralee."* Jean stood silently sobbing, but she had to be somewhat prepared for my decision. At least I prayed she was. *I wanted to climb under a rock.*

At last Angus spoke, "Freddy and Kenny, lads, I know ye have considered your options seriously and we prepared ourselves for ye decisions. We wish they be different. But now go ye, lads, wi' Godspeed and our fondest o' wishes."

I held my hand out to Jean and she accepted it. I whispered softly, "Goodbye, Jean." Tears streaked my cheeks as I said, "Darling, bonnie Jean, you will forever remain in my mind just as you are now." Jean was also crying and tears too stained her lovely soft cheeks. I felt sick and hurt all over. Never have I, nor will I ever, make a decision which will hurt me as this one has. Ken looked disheveled. He was hurting for me and for Jean. It was greatly appreciated.

I continued, "But, Jean, remember *tomorrow is another day and the sunshine of life will remain always bright.*" Momentarily, Jean responded simply, "Freddy, I wi' wait ye forever." She then dropped my hand, removed a small silver ring from her finger, placed it around the little finger of my left hand and added, "*If ye ever be lost, my ring will bren ye back to me.*"

She looked at me, a look of absolute disappointment which shall forever be embedded in my mind, smiled sadly, let go of my hand, turned, and slowly but deliberately walked away. I felt as though the door on my heart had just closed; it was an awful hurt, but my decision was made.

****

It was now 4:30 PM and Angus said, "Coom ye, lads, I shall go wi' thee to yon' Easterly Bridge where ye willa depart Glen Auralee." We had been in Auralee for twelve hours, or by 2008 time we had been gone from the outside world for a little over two days, and that would take some explaining. As we walked time seemed to have stopped and the three of us remained very silent. I supposed there simply wasn't anything else to say.

When we reached the Easterly Bridge Angus said, "Go ye now, lads, an' nay look back, for if ye do Auralee will nay be where ye canna see her." With that, he shook our hands, turned and began his walk back across the bridge. We both said, "Goodbye, Angus." But there was no answer for he had already returned to his time… to Auralee.

I said, "Come on, Ken, let's go." We headed away from Auralee and when we looked back, the bridge had disappeared as had the path. Things now appeared exactly like they were when we arrived here by 2008 time, some two days ago. I looked at Ken, "Now besides finding our way home, how are we going to explain our being missing for over two days?" Then added, "First things first, however, let's find our way out of here." As we proceeded in an easterly direction things which had seemed confusing now seemed familiar to us. As we walked toward where we left our vehicle our predicament sunk in. What are we to say to everyone who for two days have been searching for us? We decided to just play it straight and dumb.

In Penoaken over two days had elapsed, but according to our watches running on Auralee time, only 18 hours had gone by. There were several substantial facts to corroborate our story. We still had a portion of our food and water left in our knapsacks, we had our freshly killed birds, and our whiskers had only grown on Auralee time. Further where could we possibly have been for two days? So, *that's our story and we're sticking to it.*

Finally, I remembered my cell phone. I gingerly dialed the number for the Travis Inn at Penoaken. It was now 11:00 AM. It rang, and rang, and rang until after what seemed an eternity a familiar female voice answered. It was Lori! I said, "Lori, this is Fred. We were lost but have found our way back to where we left the vehicle, but it is gone." Lori shouted, "Fred, ye have been missen for two days now. We had given up hope, o' seeing ye again. Where hah' ye been to?" I replied, "Two days…we haven't been missing two days! We were lost yesterday afternoon and decided to spend the night in the woods. That's all. Can you come and fetch us?"

Lori was very excited, she shouted, "Ye stay right where ye be and we will come to ye immediately. I will get Henry." I replied,

"Thanks, Lori, and hurry. We are hungry, thirsty, need a bath, and need badly to get to *The Pub*." I told Ken we couldn't eat the small amount of food left as it was part of our story.

As we waited for Henry and Lori we agreed we would make arrangements to leave for Chicago at our earliest opportunity. We wanted to avoid questions.

When Henry and Lori arrived they immediately jumped on us with "Where in this world hah' ye been? We hah' been sick wi' worry of ye whereabouts." As I explained to Lori earlier, "We haven't been anywhere, only lost for last night." "But, Fred," Henry snorted, "this be May 16th and ye left here on May 14th." I looked at my watch, showed it to Henry, and the date read May 15th . I showed him our other evidence, said we had no idea of what two days he was referring to, and there was nothing else we could say. Henry added he was sorry but the authorities would want to talk to us. I told him fine, but this was all there was to it.

The following morning I called the airline and changed our bookings to the next available flight to Chicago which was at 11:00 AM on the 18th. On the 17th the local Constable arrived to talk with us about our *mysterious disappearance* and *sudden reappearance*. I related our story to Constable Coffee, "It was never to us at all mysterious. We got lost, stayed all night in the woods, and found our way home the next day. As for the *mysterious* two days, we simply have nothing to add, and certainly no explanations of anything unusual.

"Further, we are leaving tomorrow morning for home in order to avoid all this attention for something we know nothing about. This experience has ruined our stay here in Penoaken and we no longer feel welcome. We are sorry. That's all we have to say."

With that we packed our bags, went to *The Pub,* said goodbye and thanks to Scotty, and enjoyed a fine meal in the dining room. We thanked Lori and Henry when they stopped by to offer their apologies saying, "We still dinna understand what happened but, Sirs, know ye will always be welcome at the Travis Inn at Penoaken."

We said, "Thanks, Henry and Lori. We don't hold you to blame for anything. Whatever the misunderstanding as to what, if anything, happened, we are just chalking it off to a new bit o' *Scottish Lore*."

****

Our flight to Chicago was uneventful, drank a couple glasses of wine, ate a good meal, read all the plane material, worked the crossword puzzles, and grabbed a little shut-eye. We couldn't really talk of our experience for fear we would be overheard and people would think we were daft. On landing I did comment to Ken, "Well, it's back to the ole rat race." He just looked at me and said, "Oh, hell yes, and I can't wait."

Arriving home we immediately called our offices and advised them we would be returning to work tomorrow morning; our vacation was cut short because we simply got lonesome for our work. They all got a good laugh at that one. I hoped we could let it lay there.

I called Samantha, and to say the least she was surprised. "Oh, Fred, I am so pleased you are back so soon; what happened?" My answer was short. "Nothing really, Sam, and that was part of the problem. We just found out Scotland was not the fun trip we had hoped for." Sam hurried on, "Oh, swell, Fred, there is a huge bridge game at the club this weekend and now we can be partners. Isn't that grand?"

I thought, *Oh, hell, I haven't been back four hours and already Sam and the rat race are taking me over.* But she had trapped me and all I could say was, "Great, Sam, fine, swell, just great"

I don't know why, but my last thought of the day was, *Perhaps to smile, perhaps to cry.* I just turned over and said to myself, *Thank you, Bard.* Soon slumber arrived, at least I think it did.

****

Yet in my dream this night I was still in Auralee recounting my goodbyes to Jean…*that smile, that voice, the way she glided across the floor, and the look she had when I told her I was leaving.* Visions to be recalled for the rest of my life…and perhaps beyond. I had experienced a trip in *the fourth dimension,* and now had to rely on the *fifth dimension…imagination….* Goodnight Jean, bonnie Jean.

CHAPTER 8

LOST IN THE SHADOWS OF THE PAST

ONDAY, MAY 20th, my first day back at work was upon me. Hadn't been away long enough to have forgotten the routine. Same commute each morning, same commute each evening, same stuff in my inbox, and the same events every weekend. My fellow workers greeted me, some with astonishment that my return was so sudden. When asked why that was, I just shrugged and said, "It was not the great time we had hoped for." Fortunately there were a couple of days before anything significant was scheduled for me to concentrate on; thus, I worked to clear a significant backload of letters and reading material, but my mind kept wandering back to Auralee and Jean.

I called Ken, found he was busy doing much the same things, and invited him to do lunch in my office next week on Thursday if that was good. He readily agreed and I asked if he would be at the club this weekend. He was quick to answer, "Of course, ole buddy, let's have a beer or two."

I explained, "Sorry, Ken, no surprise to you, but my time is all assigned from Friday night until Sunday evening playing in a Bridge tournament with Sam." He responded, "Didn't take her long did it, ole pal." After we hung up, I looked in the mirror in my office and said, *Yeh, Ken, you are right, here I go again. Damn it, Fred, you have got to get out of this confounded double headed rat race…but how can you do it?*

Our Bridge game didn't fare too well. We finished in the middle of the field, an entire weekend wasted. I had difficulty concentrating, and Sam spent too much of her verbal efforts socializing rather than on bidding. When she complained about our finish, I rushed to her aid with, "Sam, not your fault. It was mine. Let's just forget it."

The following Thursday came very slowly. At noon Ken arrived at my office and good ole dependable Shirley took our orders for lunch. After she left, I asked Ken, "My friend, are you doing alright?"

He said very lackadaisically, "I guess so, why do you ask?" I countered, "You don't seem inspired." Ken responded, "You got that right." I continued, "Ken, I too am getting quite concerned about myself. Can't sleep at night or get my mind off Jean and Auralee. What you see here is not the same person who was here before our trip and that's scary. Even my outlook on life has changed. I now want the serenity, the peacefulness of a quiet rural place, everything that in my youth I felt was boring and sluggish. My demeanor is morphing into something very different."

We bantered our concerns about until time to get back to some semblance of work. Ken suggested we do this again the following week to see how things looked by then and I quickly agreed, "Same time, same station?" He said, "Yep." God, was I happy to have Ken around to relate to, or it would be very lonesome around here. Happily I considered relief would soon arrive in the form of the weekend, but then I quickly realized the folly of that thought.

Friday evening at the club awareness that everything was *never* changing overtook me, with a resounding *thud*. I'd barely time to catch my breath before Sam was all over me again, like a tornado through a Kansas wheat field. Once more, Bridge had gone poorly. Not only were we last, we were really last. I admitted to playing with a definite lack of enthusiasm, apologized to Sam, and promised things would be better tomorrow.

I was not sure she understood, but at least she didn't say anything. It was late and I was tired so we called it an evening. We arrived at Sam's home, I kissed her without passion, walked her to the door, said goodnight, and left. I definitely was not a happy camper.

Saturday afternoon Bridge improved; we were 5th out of 18 pairs. I was a little better at keeping my mind on the game. However during the evening session my mind on occasion slipped to Auralee and we fell to 8th place. Again my apologies were given, but they were not heartfelt. Play was not up to my usual performance. I just could not get with the program and told myself perhaps Sunday afternoon's final session would need to be my savior…. It wasn't, we finished 11th out of 17. Our overall finish for this lost weekend was to be expected…Last! Sam's comment was, "God, Fred, I'll be ashamed to show my head."

I said, "Samantha, it wasn't your fault. I wasn't ready for this competitiveness and it showed. Tell your friends anything you wish." When we reached Sam's home very few words passed between us other than goodnight. I knew now…our association had played itself out. My psyche could not tolerate my present circumstances any longer.

The next week passed sluggishly. This body walking around wasn't me and I couldn't find my real self. It was like being lost in a vacuum or something. I didn't call Sam and she didn't call me. It felt like a vacation, and in capital letters the sign said, *Brother, go ye forth and get this thing over with and soon*. During lunch with Ken on Thursday I talked to him about our circumstances and it was evident he was uncomfortable about his lifestyle too. I needed solitude to sort my situation out.

****

There was a beautiful park about twenty minutes from my home with a good sized lake, abundant trees, and ample wildlife. At night it should provide me with the peace and quiet where one could meditate. I needed to go there, and Saturday evening sounded just right. With only the thought of going there I began to feel relaxed and a little more in charge of myself. No Sam, no country club, and no pressure. I thought, *Go, boy, go for it.*

I spent several hours mulling over and over in my mind about what I should do at the park. Nothing was clear to me and my mind was still in a turmoil. I would take my small radio, turn on some relaxing music, and hoped help would be forthcoming to provide some answers which I badly needed.

Saturday evening I left my apartment and arrived at the park at about 8:30. Soon it would be dark and that was the atmosphere I wanted. I parked my car in a lighted area, and walked about a quarter mile to a grassy area where some picnic tables were located. Only one pole light offered a subdued glow and as the moon rose it was apparent it would be a moonlit night. The weather was clear, the stars were beginning to sparkle, and I could make out the tree lined lake in the distance.

Staring into the darkness became hypnotic and as I dozed off a dream, mesmerizing and convincing, materialized in my mind. I was in a place *Beyond the Arc* among the hills and heather of old Scotland, a land beyond time. I was lost and hungry for a place where contentment ruled. A place where the meaning of love and life prevailed, a place *somewhere in a time long past and it was beckoning me.*

Suddenly, I realized this was the place Ken and I had visited...it was Auralee! Nervousness and trepidation overtook me. When given a choice, stay or go back, I had chosen to return to the days of my present, knowing Auralee would disappear forever back to her place beyond the arc of the stars and sky.

Tonight's dream served to reinforce my feelings that my present had no feeling, no warmth, no caring, no endearing; it had always seemed to me to be thus. Now my mistake became very clear. Why did I leave Auralee, that land beyond time? It had offered me all I had been looking for. Passionately my soul now cried out to return, but it was too late, for she was gone.

I closed my eyes and asked, *"Dear land of Auralee, let me find you once more and let me reside with you forever...in your land of peace and contentment.* I rubbed my eyes and peered intently into the night trying to decide on just what had taken place.

****

As awareness returned I tried to think on what to do next; my mind was a muddle.... Suddenly, in the distance coming from the area of the trees and lake...voices? I could hear male voices and they were singing a tune similar to a 1960's ballad titled, *Jean....* "Jean, Jean, I miss you so much...I reach out to touch you but you are gone, gone, bonnie Jean." Following a pause the voices began again...this time chanting, *"Come ye back, come ye back, come ye home to bonnie Jean."* What are these voices? What do they mean? I felt certain my dream and the voices were telling me something, but what was it? I could not be certain.

For sometime I sat rather fixed mulling over what had happened. The possibilities both scared and excited me. I was now convinced both my dream and the voices were invitations for me, and perhaps Ken, to return to Auralee.

I began walking toward the lake and really didn't expect to find anything. Yet I had to see what was or wasn't there for myself. The moon was so bright and the stars so beautiful. It was a night made for miracles if ever there was to be one.

At the lake, I looked about for some sort of a sign. Anything would do...but nothing. Only stillness greeted me. I stood for a few moments and thought, *Well this doesn't help.*

I started back toward my picnic table thinking about what had happened, when suddenly, the voices returned. Emotion took charge, so overwhelming that it froze me in place for awhile.

This time the voices came from the direction of the picnic table.... *Come ye back, come ye back, come ye home to bonnie Jean....* They came to me not once but three times and each time they were a bit louder...then, just as suddenly as they had come, stillness prevailed.

****

It was 1:15 AM as I sat down at the picnic table and turned on my radio. As I did they began to play an operatic favorite of mine, *Con te Partiro,* which in Italian translates to *It is Time to Say Goodbye.* Was this only another coincidence or was destiny telling me in one more way that my returning to Auralee was possible?

When the song finished, my mission became clear to me, and it was rock solid. *I will try to return to Auralee,* and bonnie Jean will be waiting for me as she told me she would forever do. *She is my future.* I looked down at my left hand and on my pinky finger was Jean's little silver band she had given me on the day I left. I had worn it tonight for good luck and it sparkled in the moonlight as it had never shone before. Excitement and anticipation overwhelmed me.

I told myself this decision would most likely be difficult to implement. Many rocky roads would lay ahead and they would need to be cared for delicately: my job, my parents, Samantha, and Ken. Also, what would I take with me, when should I leave, and what are my goals to be once there, and how about Ken?

It was 2:45 as I drove home. I was dead tired, but sleep would not find me this night. I lay in bed pondering what to do first and told myself, *Ken.* Take care of him first.

I called Ken Sunday morning and told him to come to my place fast as there was something of great importance to talk with him about. He sounded as if he was half asleep, but he mumbled something and said he'd be here in an about an hour…just get the coffee ready and the toaster hot. An hour later he arrived.

Excitedly, I told Ken to sit down and poured each of us a cup of hot coffee. When he was comfortable, I blurted it all out…. "Ken, I am going back to Auralee to stay. Don't ask me how, but when I do, will you go with me? Either to stay there too, or if you will not or cannot stay, then at least accompany me on my trip back to Penoaken."

Ken sat immobilized for a time before stuttering, "OK, I guess this doesn't come as a surprise to me. But, Fred, my ole friend, have you gone daft, or have you been taking a joy ride in never-never-land? You know I was there too, and felt pretty certain we could not go back. What now makes you believe you can? This reminds me of Shirley Temple's 1934 song, *On the Good Ship Lollypop.*"

I continued, "Well, Ken, I am not surprised at your reaction, but you were not with me last night; wish you had been. You would be assured I am not dreaming." And continued telling Ken in detail of my encounter with the voices and about my lifelike dream.

I asked Ken to consider what I had told him and to let me know of his decision by Wednesday. In the meantime I would be proceeding with my plans.

Ken left saying, "My ole friend, what a complicated web you are weaving. You don't give me much time to consider my options, but I'll think on them. God have mercy on us both for we are for sure *Little Black Sheep Who Have Lost Our Way.*"

CHAPTER 9

IT'S TIME TO SAY GOODBYE

AYBREAK ARRIVED on Monday. Although dead tired I mustered enough strength to shower, dress, and get to my commuter train which I boarded and promptly fell asleep. My next move would be to put my boss on notice...I would be leaving my position at the firm. Thinking to myself, *How's that for starters.*

After arriving at the office I called my boss, Dan Clark, and made a ten o'clock appointment telling him it was rather urgent. Dan was a very likeable guy, a very fair and affable boss, one of the few people I would miss.

I asked my secretary, Shirley, to bring me a pot of decaffeinated coffee. Shirley was another person worthy of liking, petite blonde of definitely Scandinavian descent; believe she said it was Danish. Perhaps in another time I might have gone for her. When she arrived with the coffee I thanked her, poured myself a cup, and leaned back and finalized my thoughts for my visit with Dan. My decision was firm, but wanted to present it in a non-offensive manner.

At ten o'clock Dan's office door was open and he motioned me to come in. I entered, closed the door, sat down, and said, "Dan what I have to tell you must be said in private." He replied, "All right, Fred, that's fine but it sounds serious. Let's have at it."

I began, rather defensively, "Thanks, Dan, for taking the time to see me. What I have to tell you isn't easy and at the beginning you should know my decision has nothing to do with you. Thanks for everything you have done for me and for all the learning experiences you have provided me here under your leadership.

"Dan, I will be leaving the firm as soon as it is convenient. I am leaving the area and the publishing field for personal reasons. I have fifteen days of accrued vacation and would appreciate receiving them as a part of any cash out payment due me. Dan, this is really all there is to say."

Dan sat, looked rather surprised for a few seconds and replied, "Wow, Fred, that's a real zinger. I am shocked, but your words spoke volumes in only one sentence, and they do sound final." I replied, "Yes, Sir, you are quite right, they are." After some additional thought, he added, "I will check with my boss and personnel this morning and give you an answer today. Is that alright?" I quickly answered, "Dan, that is fine and thanks. One more thing, here is an appraisal on Shirley. She has been a great secretary and should be considered for advancement." Dan replied, "Thanks, Fred, I would have expected this of you." I got up, smiled, said thank you again, opened the door, managed a faint smile, and nervously returned to my office. Saying to myself, *That's two down…Samantha's next.*

At two thirty my phone rang, it was Dan Clark, who said, "Fred, I have a termination date for you. It wasn't easy, the boss was not happy; however, how does three weeks from last Friday sound for your last day on the payroll? And, yes, you do have fifteen days vacation pay due you." I replied, "Great, Dan, and thank you again for being so understanding and not pressing me for answers." He replied, "You are welcome, Fred, and we will miss you. You have always done good work for us. If you ever want to talk with me more, please call."

****

Later in the afternoon I telephoned Sam and fortunately she answered. I said, "Hello, Sam, remember me? Good old Fred calling." Sam rather coolly replied, "Fred? Fred? Seems I once knew a somebody by that name." *It sounded as if a tough time was in store for me.* But I continued, "Sam, need to talk with you and soon. Might I come by Wednesday evening, say at 7:00 PM?" Her reply rather surprised me. "Why, yes, Fred. That would be just super. I am glad to hear from you." I thought, *Oh, oh, can tell by her tone, she is anticipating an apology. Well, she's in for an unpleasant surprise, but I will be as gentle as possible.* "Thanks, Sam, see you then." Over the course of the next two days I spent much of my time planning and replanning what to say to Sam, and how to say it.

On Tuesday Ken called. By now nothing could phase me, but, wait, his call managed to do just that. He screamed at me, "Fred, I've just been fired! Can you imagine that? I've just been canned. I'm coming over to your place! I'll be there at six o'clock." I was thunderstruck but managed, "Sure, Ken, come on over." Before I could say anything more, he just hung up…wow. *Ken fired, didn't even suspect he was having any trouble. This does add potential dimension to my plans.*

I packed my briefcase, left a little early, caught the commuter, was home at 5:30, checked my beer and wine supply, and assured myself the bar was sufficiently supplied. Figured it was highly probable we would need it. I prepared my rollaway bed in case it might be called into service.

Not surprisingly, Ken was on time. It was evident he wanted badly to talk his problem out and I needed just as badly to listen. He grabbed himself a beer and said, "Well, Fred, I have been afraid this was coming for some time. As you know my department has been purchased by an overseas company. They offered me a lower level job which required a move overseas…turned them down! Then…they offered me a $25,000 cash separation settlement, plus three weeks pay in order to locate other work…took it! I was sick of that job anyway, but now what do I do?" Before I could reply, he continued, "Regarding your asking me to go with you to Scotland. I will do so…and, Fred, I must think more on it, but the thought of staying there, if you stay, doesn't sound totally like a bad alternative any more. Let's talk more on it."

I answered, "You weren't really fired, Ken, but your decision to leave seems final. I'm pleased you will accompany me to Scotland, and, Ken, I can only pray you will stay in Auralee with me. That is, if we manage to find her again and be welcomed." He said, "Keep me informed of your comings and goings. I am interested."

****

Wednesday would be very busy with many details, not unimportant of which was finalizing what to say to Sam. When the time to leave arrived, I jumped into my car, sped over to her place, and at 7:00 PM knocked on her door. Sam opened it, smiled politely, and motioned for me to come in. I entered, she led me to the sitting room, and motioned for me to sit on the large beige sofa.

Usually Sam would have joined me, but this evening was different. She coolly seated herself across the coffee table from me, sat quietly, and rigidly waited for me to open the conversation. I thought to myself, *Fred, she's waiting for an apology, move it ahead quickly, now's the time for the rubber to meet the road. Say something and don't stutter.*

I cleared my throat once and began, "Sam," cutting right to the point…."I am leaving soon on a venture which will take me far away from here to a place you have not heard of, and I shall not be coming back! Please don't ask me for details for I can not give you any. It is of my choosing to do this, Sam, and can only tell you it is a place where I can be myself, unlike here where only conformity and structured life prevail. You relish this lifestyle, Sam, but I immensely dislike the artificiality of it."

It was apparent Sam heard me. Her lips slightly parted, her eyes opened wide, and she appeared flushed. I continued, "Sam, a little of you will go with me. Memories of your smile, visions of your beauty, and remembrances of the many hours we spent together will always abide within me…but, Sam, you must know that in the long term we could never have a good life together. Our lifestyles and values live on different planets. Therefore, dear Sam, *It is Time to Say Goodbye*…and, Sam, sometimes please be kind to me in your thoughts."

She sat expressionless for several minutes before speaking. Letting my words settle she appeared almost serene. Finally a slight smile crossed her face as if realization of something I said must have just touched her.

She said, "Fred, there is no way I can recover from this shock right now, but thank you for your honesty and sincerity. I have a feeling you are correct in your assessment of our relationship. Yes, it is true we are miles apart in our outlook on life. I am very practical and pragmatic where you are carefree and often a bit introspective. I loved you for those qualities, but maybe you are right…perhaps it is time to say goodbye! I will be unnerved for awhile, but I'll get over it and always think of you with kindness in my heart. I wish you well on your new venture, whatever it is. Will I ever hear from you?" My reply was simple. "No, Sam, you will not."

Well, the visit wasn't exactly viewed by me exactly the same way it was viewed by Sam, but if that view worked for her, it will work for me…*c'est la vie.* When leaving her house, I turned and said, "Samantha, please feel free to tell your friends at the club you dumped me for whatever reasons you choose."

On my drive home I had a feeling of almost uncontrollable freedom, like escaping from the confinement of a maximum security gulag. At first I experienced a feeling that somehow I had been unfair to Sam. But a little voice said, *Oh, Fred, don't fret. She only used you as a convenient expedient to pursue her own agendas.* I knew, the little voice was right…goodbye, Sam. Now there were only two more important people to talk to, my mother and father.

****

I thought over and over about how best to go about telling mom and dad. I was never closely attached to my family, having left home at the start of my college years. I loved them, but their commitment to a lifestyle fenced in by their rural roots and mentality, had stymied my wanting to wander. Now I am seeking those same things in another world!

I flip-flopped between a telephone call and visiting them, but it struck me that a telephone call would be the cowardly way out. So be it, a personal visit. I called mom and asked her if she and dad, and perhaps Sue Ellen, would be home on Saturday. "I want to come down and tell you something; and no, I'm not getting married." Mom laughed and said they would be home. She continued, "It will be nice to see you, it has been over six months since you last were here." After apologizing, said I would be there at 10:00 AM. (All the while hoping for one of her classic country meals.)

No matter how hard I tried to plan for what to say and how to say it to them, my game plan just kept coming back to me like scrabbled eggs in a frying pan. Guess it will be, say what comes into your mind and pray it comes out right.

I thought about Ken and how convenient, yet how sad it was, he had no family to tell. He was an only child of a dysfunctional mother and father. His father abandoned him and his mother when he was five, so he didn't really know him. His mother remarried a traveling salesman a few years later when Ken was in his early teens. She too disappeared leaving Ken with an aunt who cared for him, but provided minimal tender-loving-care. He seldom hears from her.

Saturday morning arrived. God, how I hated to face mom and dad, but there was no evading this chore, so away I went, arriving at their front door right on time, 10:00 AM. Mom, dad, and Sue Ellen were anxiously awaiting my arrival with great expectations about what was so important to tell them.

After exchanging greetings we all took a seat in the living room, discussing every trivial subject there was: the weather, the political situation, the war in Iraq, you name it. Mom excused herself, as she was busy preparing lunch, and at eleven o'clock announced, "Come and get it." Up until now my appetite had trotted off down the road, but the aromas emanating from the table and kitchen were working hard at bringing it back. My wish had come true and we settled in for a sumptuous meal, fried chicken, mashed potatoes, biscuits, giblet gravy, and homemade apple pie. When we finished I said, "Mom, there is no way in the world that I could ever forget my favorite meal. You do it just the best. Thank you so much."

After our great feast we returned to the living room and settled in. All six eyes were glued to my forehead. The ball, so they say, was definitely in my court. So that little voice within me said, *OK, Fred, you ole crusader, they are waiting. Do your thing.*

I nervously cleared my throat twice and began, "Mom, dad, Sue Ellen, this is the most difficult thing to say that I have ever faced and hope you can accept what I am about to tell you. But remember this is something I must do. It does not affect my everlasting love for you. It is something on which my future happiness depends.

"The *crusader* is going away…to a land far away, from where I will not return. And no, mom and dad, be assured I am not dying…only going away to begin a new life. I have resigned my position at work and will be leaving soon. I will take little with me, only a few items of clothing and perhaps a few photos and small mementos. I can not tell you of this place, but you would very much approve of it. There is little else to say except to convey my non-ending love for you, and to say goodbye. I must go now and please don't come with me to my car."

I got up, hugged and kissed mom and Sue Ellen, hugged and shook hands with dad, quickly and quietly left. They were so shocked they had not yet began to cry and were unable to find words. I felt terrible, but there simply was no easy out for me. My future was now determined and there was no changing my mind now.

On my way out of the house, I had given dad an envelope with additional information; my phone was disconnected, my mail stopped. There was no way to reach me. Well, it was over; I sobbed most of the way back to Chicago.

****

I had stopped my lease and moved to a small flat near the airport; only Ken knew my whereabouts. I now had a new cell phone; only Ken knew the number. Upon returning to my flat I called Ken and before I could say anything he blurted out in a very loud voice, "Fred, *I am going with you to Auralee!*" I was ecstatic saying, "Ken, great, I was hoping you would decide to do that. It will make a huge difference in both our lives. Get on over here tomorrow morning. A new dawn has just dawned, and Kenny, me lad, we have much thinking and planning to do."

CHAPTER 10

PREPARATIONS

Today is June 20th; a little over one month has passed since our return from Scotland, and so much has transpired. Time has now arrived for the rubber to meet the road. No more goodbyes, no more looking back, only a lot of thinking, planning, and plain old work lay ahead of us.

Ken arrived at 8:15 AM with a huge smile on his face, a very pleasing sight to see. I said, "Come on in, Ken, and sit here at the table; I'll pour you a cup of coffee. Had your breakfast?" He answered, "Yup."

"Ken, I can not tell you how your decision to return to Auralee pleases me. It adds an entirely new dimension to this venture. It is now not just my trip back in time, it is now our trip. What made you decide to go, Ken?"

Taking a mighty swig of coffee he contemplated his answer. "Fred, it was a whole combination of things. Of course, my being let go was the final straw; yet, there were other reasons too. You know I had been unhappy with my general status at work, and wasn't enjoying my social well being either." Chuckling, he continued, "Perhaps Heather will still be there; kinda liked her. Also, didn't feel I was contributing anything to society here. Who knows maybe there will be more for me to offer in the eighteenth century. And finally, I didn't want to lose you. We belong together, ole friend, we belong together."

I continued, "Well, thank you for the compliment, Ken, and I whole heartedly return it. I have been hoping beyond hope you would decide to come to Auralee with me. I'm confident we'll not be sorry for making this choice.

"However, we can't just show up without a game plan, do you agree?" He replied, "Absolutely, Fred, I have been thinking the same thing. So where do we begin?" "Ken, for starters, here is a very preliminary list of items that we should consider. Let me get your take on them." He answered, "Great, go for it." I started reading my notes:

"1...We each must choose a vocation. I don't believe either of us want to be a farmer as previously you so succinctly put it. You don't want to plant seeds for a living do you? We should use our twenty-first century educations and experiences for more than planting seeds.

"In what areas would we have the most to offer: medicine, healthcare, teaching, engineering, construction, hygiene or what?

"2...Of paramount importance, what, if any, might our interface be with the twenty-first century? Will we be able to leave Auralee and then return with supplies for our work?

"3...What recreational activities might we introduce or enhance: golf, checkers, chess, croquette, various card games (whist, pinochle, solitaire, hearts, spades), etc? I even thought of something way out.... Build a twenty foot sloped wooden runway where little wooden race cars we could construct might run down it. Could become an exciting event for the folks at

Auralee, especially when accompanied by some awesome stories provided by us.

"4...Can we improve on such things as agriculture, insulation of homes, water purification and distribution?

"5...What materials might we take with us to Auralee? Things such as: pencils, paper, chalk, chalkboards, medical and health supplies, books, memorabilia, etc?

"6...We'll need to convert our cash to dated gold dollars. Should we be able to interface with the twenty-first century, hopefully over time they'll increase in value as collectibles.

"7...When should we leave for Scotland, and should we return to Penoaken as our starting point? My suggestion is we leave before the end of August and return to Penoaken. We will need help if we find it possible to return to the twenty-first century. Henry and Lori would make reliable confidants." Ken was quick to agree saying, "Besides I love that Scottish ale."

"8...We should become familiar with living conditions as they existed in 1757 such as: lighting, heating, cooking, toiletries, medicines, etc."

I continued, "Ken, these are my initial thoughts and we'll need to work on them, and I need your thoughts and input. Also, you should begin your preparations by ending your lease and moving into this apartment building so we will be more available to each other." Ken agreed he would move right away. He also concurred with my end of August timeframe, saying, "The quicker the better. Let's get started." I said, "Great, Ken, that's the attitude. Give all this some thought and let's meet here two days from now at 9:00 AM, to find out where we are."

I had decided to specialize in hygiene and medicine. Primarily, I would take over-the-counter medicines and light weight reference materials. It would depend on whether or not we were able to interface with future times to obtain ongoing supplies. Without electricity more sophisticated drugs would be out of the question.

As for Ken, I thought he might zero in on teaching. He had done a lot of instructing and lecturing at work, seemed to have a talent for it, and enjoyed it. Educating and developing assistants to help in both our areas of endeavor would be paramount.

For the next two days I spent a majority of my time browsing libraries for volumes covering the 1750's. I checked out books which offered me insights and copied pertinent pages for future reference. On the 22nd when Ken returned, I asked, "Well, Kenneth, where are we?" I told him what I had found at the libraries, while he proceeded to tell me of his efforts over the last two days.

After a couple hours of head bashing, I exclaimed, "Hey, ole buddy, it's Pizza time and it's on me. Let's be on our way to Pizza Hut where we can pig out at the All You Can Eat Buffet. He responded, "OK with me and promise to eat only three slices, or maybe four or five, or…" I interrupted him saying, "Oh, shut up. I already know you're an automatic Pizza eating machine. Hey, that reminds me, where in the hell are we going to get our Pizza in *Auralee*? Guess we'll need to figure out how to make it won't we?" He laughed and said, "Yep, we've identified challenge numero uno, and I shall take charge of it, now let's go have Pizza."

After lunch we returned to my apartment and discussed more possibilities. Over the next several days we continued to refine our plans until they were in pretty good shape, kinda like they were holding water. It was now time to begin implementation. If there ever was a time-of-essence, we were about to meet it. We were fortunate we had great resources available.

I suggested a target date to leave for Scotland. "How does August 20th sound? That gives us two months to develop ourselves within our chosen fields and to select what items to take with us." Ken responded, "Well, that will be a challenge, but I imagine we would never be ready if there was no urgency. Let's do it!" I suggested, "We need to consolidate our list of items, and continue to update them. Keeping in mind size and weight of everything we want to take will be of utmost importance."

****

Ken's acquaintance, Patricia Hart, school teacher with twenty years experience agreed to work with him in selecting supplies and teaching aides. Of course he never revealed the real meaning behind wanting to know all this. He explained by telling her he was preparing a paper for an advanced degree on surviving in an earlier time where there would not be access to modern day conveniences. I did the same with Dr. Robert Smith and Wanda Collins, two of my consultants. Our story seemed believable, but this had to be the best kept secret since D-Day.

My good friend, Dr. Robert Smith, internist, graciously offered to counsel me on emergency and minor surgical procedures, and Wanda Collins, a pharmacist, would help me with over-the-counter medicine selections. I made arrangements with Dr. Smith to spend time at his clinic learning to use various medical instruments which I might need. I also spent time with Wanda Collins, in an effort to develop my want list which far outstripped my could take list.

Ken also kept busy. Pat Hart had created a classroom consolidation agenda for teaching children by age groups. That would save space and maximize teacher's time: ages (6-8), first, second, and third grades, (ages 9-11), fourth, fifth, and sixth grades, (ages 12-14), seventh, eighth, and ninth grades, (ages 15 plus) upper schooling.

****

Meanwhile I continued to spend time with Dr. Bob at his clinic, and studied common ailments which in Auralee I would expect to encounter: colds, viruses, infections of all sorts, sprains, broken bones of the hands, arms, ribs, and legs. I learned to make rudimentary splints from tree limbs, casts made from stiffened cloth, learned the basics of appendectomies, and the removal of adenoids and tonsils. All ailments common to children, but not limited to them.

However, to adequately perform any surgery other than minor ones, I needed anesthesia such as ether or chloroform as well as painkillers like morphine and codeine. Should I not be able to obtain these medicines, as well as antibiotics, these procedures could not be performed

****

Ken detailed his recreational plans which included: card games, board games, athletics, fishing tournaments, cooking, dancing, and arts and crafts. Ken wanted to add ale drinking, but decided we already knew who the winner would be, so a contest would be for nothing. His planned recreational activities would help keep the population, both young and old, occupied during their free time.

Next I offered my list of medical paraphernalia: blood pressure apparatus, stethoscopes, minor surgical kits and materials such as clamps, surgical gloves, and a layman's medical dictionary. This was followed by a list of miscellaneous materials: pencils, paper, notebooks, paper punches, mechanical pencil sharpeners, assorted paper clips, boxes of chalk, small chalkboards, solar calculators, solar flashlights, English dictionaries, a thesaurus, magnifying glasses, compasses, scissors, sharpeners, Scotch tape, stainless steel rulers, yardsticks, Elmer's glue, weather thermometers, etcetera. Also I had my list of over-the-counter medicines. Items like Aspirin, Ibuprofen, Tums, cough medicines, stool softeners, nose and eye sprays, decongestants, petroleum jelly, Preparation H, hydrogen peroxide, hydrochloric acid, and Neosporin.

I continued to spend time at Dr. Smith's Clinic, strengthening my knowledge of the medicines available to me. Medicines, along with splinting, setting broken bones, minor surgical procedures, and hygiene will be my major specialties. If I can solve the problem of obtaining some prescription drugs, I'll be able to expand my work. If not, I'll just do my best.

****

After a few weeks a lot of water had flowed over our dam-of-learning and we decided to take a few days off for some playtime. We were doing so well even advancing our departure date was considered. I told Ken, "Let's, have some fun. For starters let's show up at the club, just long enough to be noticed, and then dissappear." Ken's eyes lit up and he chuckled, "God, let's do it, Fred. We'll have a couple drinks, play it cool, and watch what happens when we are spotted. The next day we can go to a Cub game at Wrigley Field. I'll miss those magnificent losers." I said, "Ken, you are on, go Cubbies! Cubs win! Cubs win!"

I took a couple beers from the refrigerator and we continued to discuss what to do for our "vacation." We decided to reconvene our planning July 10th. In addition to our country club visit and a trip to Wrigley Field, what else might we do?

I offered the idea of spending a couple days at a golf course, including dinner. Ken agreed and added the idea of taking a couple days off apart from each other. Sleep in and do just any old thing that comes to mind. After all in the coming days, months, and years we may be living at very close quarters. I said, "Kenneth, me boy, that earns you first place in the best of today's ideas contest."

****

The Saturday night surprise visit to the country club was our first agenda item. I picked Ken up at 6:00 PM. On the way we laughed at what we were doing and I said, "Is there anything special or do we just appear and act like a couple of specters?" Ken replied, "Fred, I rather like being mysterious and distant. If any contact is made, eye contact or otherwise, let it be them who notice us. We'll just *float* around and ad-lib it." I smiled and answered. "Great, Ken, you are about to win a second consecutive good idea prize. Let's do it."

We arrived at the club, parked the car, and entered by the front entrance. We were recognized by the doorman; he smiled and said, "Good evening, Mr. Effington and Mr. Mitchell." We flipped a nonchalant wave and strode inside as if we owned the place. Our first visit was, *sure you guessed it*, to the bar where Ken ordered a beer and I had a glass of Pinot Grigio.

The time was 6:30 PM and we could see Samantha's table from our elevated seats overlooking the dining room. There she was at her table for six, beautiful in her best belle reigning magnificence. I didn't recognize the gentleman she had in tow. He was new to her spider-like web and for some reason I felt a bit sorry for him. The other four were in her clique and she was welcome to them.

At this moment my life seemed to be fun, open, and free. I turned to Ken and said, "Gadzooks ole boy, I say, it is certainly spectacular to be here this evening. What say we be taking a walking tour of this ole joint?" Ken replied, "Aye aye, my man, let us be on with it. Will you lead, or shall I?" I retorted, "Oh my, ole compadre, it shall be me at the head of this invasion…*charge!*" We got up, took our glasses and headed into the abyss of the spider. We walked slowly and deliberately waiting for Samantha to notice us. I relished my sneaky approach into her den. The neat part of this caper was I had no preconceived idea of what to do or say.

At about eight tables off my port bow eye contact was made. It was like a broadside had just splashed down close abeam. I fired a short glance back. It was only a warning shot to place her on notice of my presence in her territorial waters. *What next, commodore?* I snapped a command back to my trailing escort, the USS Effington, "Hey, Ken, protect my rear." He replied, "Aye, aye, Skipper, go for broke."

On my way I proceeded cautiously stopping at a couple of tables, saying hello to folks whose names I could not recall. Anything to prolong my approach to where Sam was holding forth. When we reached her table, I said, "Hello, Sam." As we slowly walked by I touched my fingers to my forehead as a gesture signifying recognition.

We finally stopped near the entrance to the cocktail lounge...and waited. I had no idea what Sam might do. However, I ventured a guess she couldn't stand ignoring this scenario for long without doing something. Following a couple more eye contacts she arose and sauntered provocatively toward us. I looked at Ken, said, "OK, ole buddy, it's time to leave me on my own." He replied, " Yeh, I best be outa here...good luck."

As Sam neared she smiled graciously and said, "Hello, Fred, it is so great to see you again. I have missed you. Are you back from your venture?" My reply was gentle, yet left no doubt about my status. I said, "Sam, you look lovely as you always do. I miss you too, Sam, no, Sam, we have not as yet left, and this visit will be my last. Ken and I will be leaving very soon. We have been clearing up loose ends. Besides it looks as if you have already replaced me. Is he a bridge player?" She continued, "Yes, Fred, Steve is a Silver Life Master." (1,000 plus Master Points) "We play an excellent game together."

I continued, "Well, you should be pleased, Sam, after the many beatings you absorbed with me as your partner." Sam pushed on. "Now, Fred, it wasn't *always* your fault. Now, tell me where are you going? You have never told me." Her graciousness was not becoming her, but I replied, "No, I did not tell you, Sam, but here in this envelope is the best explanation I can give you.

"Take it, read it, and do with it as you see fit. Tonight is really goodbye and I am truly pleased at seeing you this last time." With that I leaned over, lifted her chin, and kissed her gently on the lips. "That's for the good times, Sam." She looked right at me, managed a slight smile, and stuttered softly, "Thank you, Fred." You know for once I felt she was sincere.

She took the envelope and headed for her table. I turned and disappeared into the cocktail lounge to scrape up Ken saying, "Let's leave here before Sam reads my note, perhaps we can hit a couple of our old watering holes on the way home."

****

Sam returned to her table and of course could not wait to read my note. She opened it immediately and read it. Her reaction was spontaneous. "*Oh, my God, oh, my God!*" She left my note laying on the table and went running for the cocktail lounge. Finding Ken and I had already left she rushed out the door screaming, "Fred, please come back, or take me with you." She couldn't find me so she collapsed and had to be carried to a private office and laid on a lounge while a doctor was paged. By this time my note had been read by all others at her table:

Dear Sam,

> *Maybe I'll go away up far*
> *and find a home on a distant star*
>
> *Or perhaps I'll travel a timeless sea*
> *to find the place I want to be*
>
> *Whether for me you be happy or sad*
> *Forever remember, Sam, the love we had*

Sam soon recovered sufficiently after her crowd claimed her "devastated" body, handed her my note, and began immediate counseling. Sam would recover and go on with her life. We heard about this episode from a mutual friend who was there when she put on her marvelous act. Didn't surprise me or probably anyone else, for that matter.

****

During the next two days we played golf at a nice course nearby. We found a twosome made up of two retired gentlemen who we played for a dollar a hole. Ken and I won two dollars the first day and broke even the second…wow, what a victory. Our celebration was short lived; however, since the winner had to buy a round of beer. Kind of like a mouse that roared scenario. We had fun, all that counted.

Next came Wrigley Field, home of those lovable, flubbable Chicago Cubbies. I truly will miss these guys who are trying for the hundredth year to win it all. The world isn't ready for it, so we will hope their ineptitude reigns gloriously on forever!

It was now July 6th and my final four days of "vacation" was spent watching television, going to the movies, and eating waffles and hamburgers, some of the things which shall be missed. It was rather like saying farewell to the twenty-first century.

Additionally I did spend a lot of time planning my agenda for the 10th when Ken and I would reconvene. I concluded that we should step up our departure date to August 7th.

****

July 10th dawned. The first item was gaining Ken's agreement on the 7th. I asked him; he agreed. We were anxious to proceed. We began organizing the items we would take with us to Scotland, each taking two large suitcases, one carry-on case each, and a tote bag. They would contain our clothing, personal items, and some of our medical and teaching supplies.

On August 1st I placed a call to Henry Travis at the Inn at Penoaken. Fortunately he and Lori were both there. I said, "Hello, Henry, this is Fred Mitchell and hopefully have exciting news for you. Ken Effington and I would like to visit you again at the Inn. Could we have our old rooms back starting August 8th for, say a week?"

Lori was on an extension, checked the room availabilities, and said graciously, "Yes, Fred, they are available and we will hold them for you. We can hardly wait to see you two." Henry entered his agreement, saying, "Yes, there be so many questions."

I replied, "Henry, Lori, we are sure you have questions, but one extremely important limitation is attached to our visit. You can not, I say again, can not divulge our coming to Penoaken. We'll explain more *to only the two of you* when we arrive. Should anyone else find out, we will have to immediately cancel our trip and return to America. Have I made these conditions clear? And, can you agree to them?"

After a pause, Henry spoke. "Fred, we dinna have reason to doubt your sincerity and I dinna see reason why we canna conform to your instructions. Do you agree, Lori?" Her answer was quick, "Yes, Fred, I be on your team and I do concur." I closed saying, "Great, I'm sure you will be glad you did and assure you, there is nothing shady about our coming. Unusual, but not illegal. We'll see you in my room after dinner on the evening of August 8th. Better yet, perhaps you could join us for dinner…due to the circumstances you and Lori would need to cater it, but remember we are paying the tab." Henry said, "Not a problem, Fred. We pretty much remember what ye and Ken liked, including the Scottish ale." I answered, "Thanks, Henry, thanks Lori. We will see you both soon; goodbye for now."

Next, I called the airport and ordered first class plane tickets and we were confirmed on a flight from O'Hare to Edinburgh arriving early afternoon. That left one major item. What would we do for money? We had purchased 50 twenty dollar gold pieces ($2,000) dated 2000 and earlier in the hopes they would appreciate in value. The bulk of our funds available, after disposing of all our personal things including our two cars, we would transfer to a bank in Edinburgh ($60,000). All our current expenses had been paid. Our bankroll was not a lot of money, but that's all folks, it would have to do. When it's gone, who knows.

It is now August 2nd. Only five days until we vacate ole Chicago and America forever. Our decision is irrevocable unless Auralee doesn't reappear. However, I am confident she will and we will be welcomed back. In the improbability she has closed her door to us, we shall return to Chicago and formulate other plans.

I turned to Ken and said, "OK, Tiger, what shall we do until the 7th?" Ken said, "Let's go play some more golf, visit for the last time a few of our old watering holes, drive about the city, take in the sights, and pig-out." I said, "Great, that's our plan; should we have any extra time we'll use it to once more go over the plans for our upcoming future. Let's also allow sufficient time for final packing."

Finally our time to leave arrived. The limo had already picked Ken up and now it was my turn to load up. Funny, but I had a lump in my throat. I felt as though I might cry. I was leaving forever my twenty-five years of life here for what I did not really know. My parents, siblings, friends, acquaintances, the Cubbies, golf, bridge, television, telephones, my computer, pizza, running water, indoor toilets, showers, automobiles, modern medical facilities, and so much more. Well, as Ken said, "Look out, here we come, planting seeds and all."

As the limo pulled away for the duration of the trip to the airport both of us sat and silently watched our "old" world slowly pass by and disappear behind us.... As we drove along a rather ironic twist entered my mind, *We are leaving the new world for the old world which when we arrive there will be our new world and this will become our old world.*

CHAPTER 11

SCOTLAND AFORE YE

WE ARRIVED at O'Hare Field with two hours to spare. Our check-in was uneventful and we found a couple seats near our boarding area. It didn't take Ken long before he observed, "We have not eaten for some time and our last meal in the states should be a memorable one like a McDonald's super-sized cheeseburger, French Fries, with a Diet Coke Meal Deal. We may as well go out stuffed and in style." I chuckled, "Let's go. You know an occasional visit to McDonald's is something else I will miss." We found seating available at the food service area; thus, we ordered our meals, seated ourselves, and dug into our *last supper*. After stuffing ourselves we returned to the boarding area and relaxed.

We had been operating on fast forward since leaving home and still there was time before boarding. I said to Ken, "Let's find a window that overlooks the city and absorb the sights. Kind of a way of saying our last goodbye to Illinois." Ken said, "Great."

We had difficulty finding anything to look at other than runways, parking lots, and taxis. Finally we found a good spot overlooking a small park and for awhile stood quietly, contemplating our futures. Certainly we were sad, trading our present lifestyles for those of a time long past. Doubts, I had a few. Looking at the sights before me which soon I hoped would be gone forever caused me to have more concerns; but, my resolution was absolute. *My mind was locked in overdrive. We are on our way to a new life and there can be no sorrow or looking back.*

After about twenty minutes I said to Ken, "Seen enough?" He didn't answer right away, but finally rather remorsefully replied. "Yes, Fred, it's over…and now we are travelers on our way to, kinda like a land of our rebirth. May God help us." He smiled, and we returned quietly to the boarding area where we now had less than a half hour before takeoff. We continued to sit in abstract silence.

When the boarding announcement arrived we were transfixed in a kind of stupor. *Never mind how we had prepared ourselves over the last few weeks, never mind how we had told each other we were grown men ready for a new life, never mind any of that stuff… suddenly we were petrified.*

As we boarded our plane perspiration was evident on my forehead. I felt hot and wiped my brow with my arm. Ken was rather glassy-eyed and his mouth was slightly open but we nervously proceeded onboard and located our seats in the last row of the first class section. After we adjusted our carry on luggage and sat down, Ken turned to me and said rather cautiously, "Can't wait 'till the drink service begins, need a pepper-upper."

Suddenly, a voice announced, "Fasten your seatbelts, turn off all electronic equipment, and store your trays in their upright positions." I'd heard that announcement many times, but there was something rather final sounding about it this time. I gritted my teeth and muttered, "Oh, hell, Ken, the time has arrived."

The big plane taxied into takeoff position, the jets roared, and we raced down the tarmac. Buildings and scenery raced by… the nose of our giant bird suddenly angled upwards, the wheels thudded into their up positions, and reality again hammered home. I looked at Ken and strangely he appeared serene as if this was only another normal takeoff. I said, "Ken, you OK?" He replied "Uh huh, couldn't be better. The drinks here yet?" Couldn't help but smile, chuckled a bit, and replied, "Nope, but it won't be long" Personally my heart was racing, I felt a mixture of exhilaration and fear all at the same time. I leaned back, took a deep breath, and thought, *Well, we were finally on our way to today's yesterday.*

Our flight attendant (remember the good ole days when she was a stewardess) brought us a tray of snacks, left the dinner menu, and took our drink orders. We each requested a very dry martini. Her nameplate read Michelle, she smiled graciously, said, "Thank you, Mr. Mitchell, Mr. Effington. It is my pleasure; let me know when you need anything else." In a few minutes our martinis arrived and Michelle covered our trays with a linen cloth before placing our drinks in front of us. Ken picked his drink up and offered a toast. "Here's to the first, may it not be the last." I offered, "Here's to one more, and it will be our last…tonight." He laughed and said he agreed.

We finished our first martini and asked Michelle to bring us one more. As we savored our second one, she took our orders for dinner. Ken selected a filet mignon and I chose chicken cordon bleu.

While waiting for our meals, Ken said, "Fred, I'm still quite uncertain about some things. I just can't convince myself that it is a given slam-dunk we will be able to return to Auralee." After thinking about what to say I responded. "Ken, understand your concerns and can't guarantee it either. However, had you been with me at the park that evening I told you about, you might feel a lot more confident that we shall be able to return." He responded, "Yeh, probably would."

Ken continued, "How about Henry and Lori? What will you tell them and are you absolutely confident they can keep our secret?" I replied, "Ken, the second question is easy. Yes, I have absolute confidence in Henry and Lori. Without their help we would be unable to return occasionally from Auralee; we would be unable to obtain new supplies. Concerning your first question, I've given a lot of thought as to what to say. Please just let me do the talking. If two people get involved it will only add confusion. Don't you agree?" Ken thought for a moment and said, "Yes, Fred, as usual, you are right. Go for it, ole buddy." I said, "Thanks, Ken, let's finish our drink, our meals will be here soon."

Michelle brought us fresh napkins, silverware, and our dinners. They looked as though they had just been prepared at a leading restaurant in the Chicago Loop. We were hungry and devoured them absolutely. When we finished, Michelle picked up the debris, brought some pillows, blankets, turned off our overhead lights, and said, "Goodnight, gentlemen, see you for breakfast."

We were tired, shut our eyes, and hoped the sandman would find us soon. In a few minutes, Ken was breathing heavily. Good news for him, but me, I had too much to think about. My mind churned and churned, repeating every thought I had considered since the day this all started. Yet before long sleep did find me, at least for a time. It became a night of doze, think, dream, wake up, doze, and so on. Not a perfect night's rest, but it would have to do.

We woke up to a new day, Michelle arrived, and said, "Good morning, Fred and Ken. How was your night?" We both groaned, but said, "Fine, what's for breakfast?" She handed us our menus and smiled. Ken selected, cheese omelet, crisp bacon, juice, toast, and coffee. For myself it was waffles, crisp bacon, two juices, and decaffeinated coffee. One thing for certain, we were not going to arrive in Scotland hungry. Once more, as we finished, Michelle collected our plates and we again thanked her.

It was late morning and we were still at sea. In about a half hour we encountered the far northern coast of Ireland, and soon we would begin our long approach leg to Edinburgh. Ken turned to me and said, "It's almost here, Fred. It's almost time. Aren't you a bit nervous?" Couldn't think of anything better to say other than, "Sure." That more or less took care of things for awhile.

Time passed quickly and as during our first trip to Scotland we watched the Irish landscape pass below us. At twenty-five thousand feet we couldn't discern much, but as we lowered our altitude to about fifteen thousand feet, small towns, pastures, and cars moving along the highways appeared. Finally the captain announced we were beginning our final approach to Edinburgh International Airport, which boosted our excitement level up several notches. Shortly we touched down, taxied to our gate, the plane stopped, and we began deplaning.

****

Next stop was the baggage area and amazingly our bags were among the first off, just like the last time. *Man, I love this airport.* Next came the car rental counter and here again all was in order as we quickly signed our papers. A young man took our bags, said "Follow me, please," escorted us to the curb in front of the terminal and placed our bags in the rental car trunk. I gave him a tip, he said, "Thanks," and we were once again on our way once more to Penoaken.

I remembered traveling this route before. Thus, I exited the airport quickly and we were on our way. We should be able to travel the distance to Penoaken in less than two hours as there really wasn't much new to see. Let's face it, both of us were anxious to get this part of the trip behind us. The *fun part* was coming up next.

We did stop for a sandwich, but otherwise pushed on. It wasn't long before we saw the sign to Penoaken and turned off the highway. Now our anticipation was really in high gear. Momentarily…there it was, the village limits, and nearby the entry road leading to the Travis Inn. We stopped, called the Inn on my cell phone, and Lori answered. I said, "Lori, this is Fred Mitchell. Ken and I are at the entrance to the lodge. We want to dodge as many people as we can, so may we enter via the back door and go straight to our rooms?" Lori responded, "Freddy, aye, ye canna come in the back door. I be certain ye will explain all this to Henry and me at supper this evening." I replied, "You bet we will, Lori, and we apologize for all this mystery." With that said, we proceeded to the rear entrance where Lori was waiting.

I parked the car, threw Lori a kiss, loaded our baggage onto a cart, and said, "Lori, Ken and I are happy to be here." She replied, "And we be glad you be wi' us too. Now we be goen quick to ye rooms." She led the way and we followed her with the baggage cart. On the way I said, "Lori, sorry to be so secretive, but after this evening you'll understand." She smiled politely, "That be fine, Freddy. Henry and I be very curious to hear ye story." She opened our rooms doors and we entered. Lori told us dinner would be served in my room at 6:30 if that was alright and I agreed it was. She smiled and left.

I turned to Ken and remarked, "Ken, you know for the first time I feel devastatingly alone. Why is that?" He replied, "Hell, I don't know just what did you expect, Fred? We are very much alone and it's going to get worse. At least for awhile we have, Lori, Henry, and I hope soon Scotty, to talk to." I continued, "You are dead right, buddy, and I'll be over this feeling soon. Go unpack and then you come back and we'll talk." Ken responded, "Would it be OK if Lori brought us each a stein of ale?" I agreed after we unpacked it would be fine, but only one.

Ken left to unpack and soon returned. I said, "Come on in and have a seat." And then continued, "Ken, as discussed before, this evening will be for me alone to tell Henry and Lori about our visit to Auralee last May, and why we have returned. There cannot be more than one spokesman. You must listen carefully to all that is said. Hope you understand." He paused for a time, finally answered, "That will be difficult for me, ole buddy, but I must agree with your reasoning. I will try diligently to be a mental recorder, and jot down a few notes to discuss with you later." I responded, "Ken, that's great, now go ahead and ask Lori if she would bring us a couple ales." He did so without delay and they were delivered posthaste. Man, did they taste good. We slowly drank them and continued to discuss the upcoming evening events. Ken then returned to his room, I took a long shower, and laid down until it was time for him to return for dinner

****

Ken knocked on my door at 6:10, opened it, and entered. I said, "Ken, sit yourself down. You know, I feel surprisingly ready for this evenings tell all. Hope the euphoria lasts." He laughed, "Well, you've got the easy part. It's me that has to keep his mouth shut; that hurts." Soon Henry and Lori arrived with the portable trays for our dinner. It took two trips before everything was ready and the last table was adorned by two bottles of a good German Moselle.

I said, "Now this looks great." I was ogling a rack-of-lamb, golden brown potatoes sautéed in a wine sauce, crisp Caesar salad, delicate biscuits with sweet butter, and for dessert apple pie with sharp cheese. The appearance was delectable and the aromas tantalizing. I said, "We're ready to eat. I know you are anxious for me to say something about why we came back to Penoaken, so let's do it." Henry poured us each a glass of wine and proposed a toast. *"To our friends from America, who on their last visit took the most amazen grouse hunt in our history."* Ken and I laughed, raised our glasses and said, "Here, here." The three of us took our seats and Henry, acting as host, delivered to us our feasts. After finishing our sumptuous meal and polishing off the last of the wine, Ken and I thanked Lori and Henry profusely.

Ken then arose, said, "OK, you two. You have been waiting for our story, so here it comes. Remember what Fred tells you is for your ears only, and *please, please* hold your questions until he is finished. It is important to his maintaining continuity. If after he finishes, you have questions or concerns, please, ask him, OK?".... They both were goo-goo eyed with anticipation. Henry and Lori both stammered at first, but then agreed wholeheartedly to comply. Ken said, "OK, here's Fred in all his red, white, and brews."

****

After clearing my throat I began what seemed to me would be a difficult task. There was no question, I had the devoted attention of my audience, all two of them.... "Henry, Lori, you recall last May 11th, the day we arrived here. After completing our check-in we spent the afternoon giving the Inn and it's surrounding gardens the once over. It was during this time that you, Lori, explained the old Scottish legend about the two grave markers that read, "Known only to God." This was our first exposure to your fabled Scottish lore; but it would not be the last. On the 12th we split our day between visits to the museum with Mac Macfarlane, and to the old Church of Scotland with Reverend Paul Seymour.

"I want to tell you particularly of our experience at the church. After our tour, I asked Reverend Seymour if we might review some of the records housed in the church library, and he kindly agreed. We randomly selected four volumes. From them, I picked 1725 and 1755 and after several hours, I stumbled on an entry which grabbed my attention...an old hunter by the name of Haggis Frisbee reported that he had found the little village of Auralee missing.... According to his report, everything had disappeared and his experience was recorded in great detail. Yet I found nothing recorded by Reverend Paul, the church priest at that time. *I did find this strange.* Also odd, the cemetery records listed Haggis Frisbee's death as May 21, 1755, the day following his report to Reverend Paul.

"The next morning Ken and I returned to the church and reread the journal together. I told Reverend Seymour about our discovery and asked if he was familiar with the report in 1755 telling of a missing village. He said he was not, so the three of us returned to the journal and opened it to the page from where we had read Haggis Frisbee's account…. *The pages were empty*…. I stared in disbelief. It did not appear any pages had been removed and was at a loss for words. What could I say except obviously I had made a mistake. Perhaps thinking me a bit daft, the Reverend took the easy course of telling me to not feel bad as mysteries wrapped in lore abound in ole Scotland.

"Confused I left to find the location of Haggis Frisbee's grave and verified he was born in 1720 and died on May 21, 1755. Now I knew, at least, Haggis was not a figment of my imagination. If you remember, Henry, I asked you if you ever heard of an Auralee or Haggis Frisbee from many years ago, and you had not." Henry nodded his head in the affirmative.

"That afternoon you, Henry, provided Ken and myself with instructions and directions for our grouse hunt. Later we packed our vehicle and at 5:30 on the morning of May 14 we were off on our great expedition. We followed your instructions to where the road ended about 9 miles from here, unloaded our gear, and began our trek.

We began our hunt at approximately 6:30 and moved through several glens and wooded areas until around 1:30 PM when we agreed it was time to find our way back to our vehicle. To our amazement we were confused about our bearings and it seemed the harder we tried to find them the more lost we became…. Obviously we were walking in circles. By 4:15 it was getting dark and in accordance with your instructions, Henry, we looked for a place to camp for the night, bedded down about 7:00, and soon dozed off.

"At around 12:45 on the morning of May 15th I was awakened by what sounded like water coursing over rocks. Ken heard the sound too. Using our flashlights we saw a path which had not been there the previous evening and followed it to a stone bridge which spanned a wide creek. At 2:00 AM we crossed the bridge and decided to wait until dawn before moving on. When morning arrived we soon could see houses, heard dogs barking, and cows mooing. Had we found civilization where none was supposed to be?

"We saw a man standing in the doorway of the nearest house dressed in eighteenth century garb. Then another appeared and gingerly we approached them and introduced ourselves by name and our being from America. We asked where we were? Their response confirmed my suspicions. The portly one told us we were in the village of Auralee in the year of our lord, 1757. His name was Angus Macgregor and the other was Mayor Robert Bright.

"If we were not dreaming, we had found the missing village referred to in the church record. I told them we were from the year 2008 and the one called Angus calmly responded, 'Oh, my, lads, ye coom a long way, be ye lost?' I answered, 'Yes, or we are dreaming?' He replied, 'It nay be a dream, and later ye will understand when we visit Reverend Dundee.'

"Angus then took us in tow and we began a walk through Auralee, passing a festival being set up in honor of their *Day of Deliverance*. As yet we didn't know what *deliverance* referred to. We then went to his home, a rather large masonry and stone structure with a thatched roof, where we were introduced to his daughters, Jean, 21, and Mary, 17. They were two of the loveliest lasses I had ever seen.

"The girls took us on a walking tour of Auralee and the little village impressed us by it's well maintained appearance. We returned to the festival where games were being played, food was being served, acrobats were performing, and to Ken's delight, they were serving heather ale.

"I talked with Jean, and asked her questions like, 'Are you happy here and what do you do to keep yourself busy?' Jean very spontaneously smiled and told me she was very happy and had many things to do, and then she added something I'll always remember….'I be happy, Freddy, but it will please me greatly if ye willa stay here wi' us…of course, if that be possible.'

"I began having strange thoughts and could not get my feelings toward Jean into a proper perspective. I asked Angus for time to talk more with her before we went to see Reverend Dundee, to which he agreed. We walked to a lovely shaded glen where benches had been placed for folk to come and relax. I asked Jean what she meant by her, hope you will stay, comment. She related to me how she had a dream that someday a proper lad would come to Auralee and be her own, and how she had a deep feeling I was that person. I told her I too had an unusual feeling of affection for her, but didn't know if I could stay in a land so different from the place from which we came, and hoped Reverend Dundee could answer some of my questions.

****

"We rejoined Ken and Angus and continued on to see Reverend Dundee. He was waiting, outfitted in his splendid kilts. Angus introduced us informing him he believed Jean and Freddy had already established an interest.

"The good Reverend told us about the miracle bestowed upon Auralee in the year 1754. It was granted at the behest of the Elder Reverend Toomley to recognize Auralee's wish to remain outside the turmoil which surrounded it.

"'God then issued unto us his divine declaration, which I canna repeat here, except to tell ye Auralee exists in parallel with your time but time passes here at a different pace.' That is why we were away for two and a half days, by Penoaken time, but only twelve hours had gone by in Auralee. Reverend Dundee asked if we had questions, and we responded, yes, but asked for a short time to consider them in light of what he had told us. He understood and we walked to the small glen where Jean and I had talked earlier."

"We discussed and contemplated, our concerns. Ken was for returning home, arguing we could not be happy *planting seeds* when we were used to cars, planes, television, and Chicago Pizza. Yet peace, contentment, and my interest in Jean appealed to me. However, I too had to question whether I could truly be happy here because if not, Jean would not be happy either. We then returned and found Angus and Jean waiting.

"The time had come to ask Reverend Dundee our questions and make our decisions known. There was no doubt in Ken's mind he was going home, and I had concluded if Reverend Dundee could not provide satisfactory answers to my questions…then I too would return home.

"When we arrived at Reverend Dundee's home I asked the good Reverend two questions. Describe for us the Land of Auralee which he did in detail. My second question was the one which really mattered the most to me. *If we decide to leave Auralee, is it possible we could return?* Reverend Dundee considered his response. I would never forget it. *'Aye, Freddy…perhaps one could return. If ye love someone enough then perhaps anything be possible. I canna speak for the Lord, it be only me thinken.'* I remember being somewhat surprised by his answer, but it at least left a small crack-in-the-door. Maybe it would be possible.

****

"The time for decision had arrived. I wanted to make my reply to Jean quick, and frame it as softly as possible. I told Jean I loved her, but because of the vast separation in time, believed neither of us would be happy, and that would not be fair to her; therefore, Ken and I would be leaving Auralee. Jean began crying, but said nothing. I wanted to crawl under a rock.

"Finally, Angus spoke, saying he knew we had considered our decisions seriously, wished they could have been different, but to go with Godspeed. Angus told us to follow him to the East Bridge and as we left Jean spoke. Very softly she said, 'Freddy, I shall waiten for ye forever,' removed a small silver ring from her finger placing it on the little finger of my left hand. She smiled that cherished smile, turned and silently walked away.

"When we reached the bridge, Angus told us to cross and to nay look back as he and Auralee would not be there. From here you pretty much know the story. We had been in Auralee for only twelve hours, but by your time we had been away for two and a half days. Ken and I felt uneasy with all the concern over where we had been. What could we say? We just packed and went home.

"A couple of months later while visiting my favorite park one evening and feeling awful about my decision to leave Auralee, I heard voices coming to me from toward the lake. They sounded like an invitation…. *Come ye back, come ye back, come ye back to bonnie Jean….* Over and over the voices beckoned me.

"Working conditions hadn't changed and neither had my relationship with my lady friend, Samantha. Also, Ken's feelings about his future wasn't improving." Thus, one day I told Ken I was returning to Scotland and asked him to come along. Ultimately he agreed; thus, we called you, and like two little black sheep who have gone astray here we are. Now you know the whole story and what remains now is how do we get back to Auralee?"

CHAPTER 12

BEYOND THE ARC

"OUR PLANS are: from the Inn we will proceed to the place where we entered Auralee last May, and assume she will reappear, but we have no guarantees. However, should we be successful, another assumption is we will be able to transit occasionally back and forth between Auralee and twenty-first century Penoaken. If these assumptions come true, we'll need an interface here in Penoaken, and we hope that will be you, Lori and Henry.

"Think very carefully about what we are asking of you and remember what we tell you must be maintained a closely guarded secret. You can not even know how we transit to Auralee. Mostly we would need your help maintaining a nominal amount of supplies. Ken and I have brought some cash and gold coins to open a joint bank account nearby.

"Also we have brought, and will purchase here, an amount of medical and teaching supplies to initially take with us to Auralee…. My expertise will be medicine and hygiene, Ken's will be teaching.

"Initially, we'll need you to transport us to the glen where we parked our vehicle last May, and we'll require two Shetland ponies to pack our supplies. The ponies will stay with us; let us know the cost. That's pretty much it, guys. If we are able to return to Penoaken, it will be with no advance warning and would be for only a short period of time, perhaps three or four days. Think diligently on all you have heard. If anything is not clear, we'll talk more tomorrow. Would my room at 1:30 PM be OK?"

Breathing hard, Henry coughed, stuttered, and said, "Fred, aye the morrow be fine. Meantime, Lori and I be thinken on what ye tell us. It be a special tale ye spin lad, but I believe ye tell us truthful. I canna be thinken o' any reason ye might have to be spinen us a fable."

****

The next morning Ken and I made our first appearance outside our rooms. We had breakfast in the dining room and following that walked to the church. The good Reverend Seymour was there. I asked if we might peruse the 1755 church journal once more, and he graciously and without question said, "Of course."

Ken and I found our way to the church library, selected the 1755 journal and opened it to the page where I had seen the entry based on Haggis Frisbee's account…. It was still not there; I turned to Ken and said, "Now someday, somehow, we are going to fix this. We owe it to ourselves and to Haggis."

We once more thanked the good Reverend, passed via the cemetery, and paid our respects to good ole Haggis. We returned to the Inn, said hello to the ducks and geese on the lake, had a cup of soup, a Diet Cola, and went to my room to rest and wait for Lori and Henry.

At 1:30 there was a rap on the door. I opened it and asked Lori and Henry to come in, take a seat, and have at us. Both were smiling and we took that as a good omen. Henry spoke first. "Gentlemen, at first both Lori and I felt we be overwhelmed. But as we talked more of ye uncanny story, the more we came to ha' ah feelen o' believen what ye tellen us be true." Lori chimed in, "Oh, aye, Freddy and Kenny, we be believen wi' ye revelation and ye can count on us. We will be helpen ye devotedly at all times."

I answered, "Thank you, Henry, and thank you, Lori. Without your help we could not accomplish many things which we hope to do in Auralee. However, in doing these things, in no way will we attempt to change Auralee. We want her to stay as she has always been. That primarily is why we wish to return there to make her our home.

"It is now 3:00 PM on August 9th and here is what we need to do. We'll set the date of August 11th as our day to leave for our attempt to relocate Auralee. Once you leave us at the glen you may assume if we have not returned to the Inn by August 17th, we have successfully reached Auralee.

"Henry, Ken and I need to open a joint savings/checking account, purchase some over-the-counter drugs, and acquire two Shetland ponies with packs on which to carry our baggage. Additionally, we need transport from here to the trail end for us, the ponies, and our baggage. We also need food for 5 to 6 days. Let us know what the costs for this will be, including our stay here at the Inn, and we will pay in cash." Henry was quick to add none of this would be a problem. He would take care of everything and shepherd us to the bank and anyplace else we needed to go.

****

August 11, 2008…our day of reckoning arrived. We did not sleep well the last night, no surprise. It was 4:30 AM; Henry and Lori were ready. At breakfast we enjoyed our last twenty-first century breakfast. No one talked much and when we finished, I said, "Well, gang it's time." We left for the truck which was already loaded with the ponies and the rest of our gear. Henry and Lori had been busy.

Our trip to trail end took thirty minutes and we arrived there at about 7:00. Our ponies and packs were unloaded and we were ready to begin our trek. We said our goodbyes and best wishes. Ken and I kissed Lori on the cheek and gave Henry a big hug. Lori was crying and Ken said, "We love you two, we'll be seeing you." That said, we grabbed the reins of our ponies, and trudged forward in search of our destiny. For sometime we didn't look back; when we did Henry and Lori had departed.

Ken looked at me and said, "Well ole buddy, I do feel a tad bit alone, how about you?" "Yeh, Ken, sorta like the astronauts must have felt on their first journey to the moon. Anticipation is stimulating, but the specter of failure is always present." Ken smiled and said, "Good analogy, ole sage"

There was about seven miles of rather rough and wooded terrain to traverse before we hoped to find the large tree stump where we previously had located our camp the evening of May 14th. Along the way we would look for a large tree which was bent at a steep angle and that would be our first indication we were on the right trail. We estimated if we could average one-mile-per-hour, and allow for three half hour rest stops, we hoped to reach our objective, the tree stump, between 3:00 and 4:00 PM.

By then it would be dusk and time to setup our campsite. We trudged onward, once more felt like the two little black sheep who had gone astray, and hoped the hand of God would guide us through our travesties. Frankly, I thought it was asking a lot from him, but figured we could use all the help we could get.

The day passed very slowly and we weren't certain we were making our desired mile-per-hour average. At first there was a little problem handling our ponies named America and Illinois. They weren't used to us and we were sure not used to them. They were professional packers, but we weren't. However, after the first hour or so our handling improved and so did our progress. We trudged on, and on, and on. Finally I said, "Hey, Ken, ain't this fun?" He looked at me and answered, "Hell, Fred, if I had a gun, I'd shoot you." We both laughed at ourselves. Onward we trudged, rested, and kept plowing along until at three o'clock Ken hollered, "Fred, over there, isn't that our old bent over tree?" I stopped and said, "You bet it is my friend. You found it. Now we know we're on the right track. Our stump can't be over a mile away. Let's take ten and push on." He nodded his head and we sat down, leaned up against a tree, and rested. America and Illinois grazed nearby; we snacked and took a good slug of water.

After about fifteen minutes we continued our effort. By now the ponies were used to us and we more or less just followed them. Fortunately they "understood" English. In about an hour we rounded a curve and a short distance ahead…our stump appeared. Funny how unusual it felt to find an old tree stump that to us looked like a haven out here in the middle of nowhere. It was 4:00 PM. I said to Ken, "How is that for navigation? Christopher Columbus should have done so well." He replied, "You know that is right, ole buddy; suddenly I feel much better."

We tethered the ponies, removed their packs, laid out our bedrolls, and ate a snack. We then retired to our stump and considered our future. It was now rather dark; as we recalled there would be little, if any, moonlight. Only our small solar flashlights would provide any light we might need. I said, "Let's tell ghost stories." Ken laughed, "You mean like when we were at Boy Scout campouts?" I replied, "Hell, no, we talked about Girl Scouts at mine."

Soon, however, we were both contemplating the arrival of some signal indicating Auralee was near. Our aura of levity soon turned into an atmosphere of more seriousness. We realized we were at the mercy of waiting, nothing else we could do.

I asked, "Ken, was Chicago, the club, and Samantha for real or are they just dreams? It seems so long ago and so far away. Auralee, Jean, Angus, Reverend Dundee, are they just dreams too? Suppose this stump, might be the only real thing?" Ken finally responded, "Fred, I love you like a brother, but damn it, man, you have a maddening way of making me think. You want to know what I think? Well for your information, I don't think any of them are real. They are all dreams, and we don't exist either except in those dreams. We are just psychogenic matter. If we ever wake up, it's all over, baby."

Wow! I had never heard Ken so philosophic. I replied, "Hey, ole friend, that's fantastic. We are only ideas floating around as figments of our own imaginations. Hey, I can handle that, but certainly hope we turn out to be more than an idea."

We continued this bantering around and it did help us pass the time. Suddenly it was 10:00 PM and still no sign of Auralee. I told Ken we just needed to be patient, it was time for a little nap, and he agreed. We headed for our bedrolls and tried to relax.

We awoke early on the 12th, ate breakfast, attended to our ponies, and walked a short distance to where last May the bridge had been; however, saw nothing which even remotely looked as if a bridge or Auralee had ever been there.

For loss of anything better to do, we took a stroll several times always experiencing the same result. In between we sat on our stump and chatted about most anything which came to our mind, snacked, and walked the ponies. The day passed extremely slow: 10:00 AM, noon, 3:00 PM, 5:00 PM, and suddenly it was dark. I will give Ken credit, not once did he proclaim his doubts.

At last, he asked, "Fred how long will we wait for some sign before we head back?" I replied, "Ken, honestly don't know, but the sign will come, and believe it will come tonight. I think we are being tested to see if we are really sincere in our desire to return to Auralee." He replied, "Fred, if it is of any value, I too sense something is imminent." At 7:00 we retired. The night was again cool and still; soon a restless sleep overtook us.

****

At 4:00 o'clock on the morning of August 13th I heard it…the sound of water coursing over rapids. I shook Ken and said, "Listen, listen, do you hear it?" We both jumped to our feet and he answered, "Yeh, by God, I hear it. The water is back and, Fred, look here, the path is back too."

We grabbed our flashlights and scurried down the path until shortly we saw the familiar stone bridge. I had a feeling of almost unimaginable delight…the entryway to Auralee was here, right in front of us.

When we neared the bridge we could see the silhouette of a man standing just beyond it. Could it be? I called out, "Angus, is that you?" He responded, "Aye, Freddy, it be Angus to welcome ye and Kenny back to Auralee.

"Coom ye across, lads, and ye be home. It be me understanden that be ye intention." I replied, "Yes, Sir, that is our intention. May we collect our baggage and cross?" He replied, "Aye, lads, and again I welcome ye." We hurried back to our campsite and loaded the packs onto our ponies. On our way back to the bridge Ken, said, "Hell, Fred, never had any doubts, always knew it would happen this way." Now it was my turn, I said, "Yup!"

We rushed across the bridge and threw our arms about Angus. In my finest Scottish accent I said, "Angus, ye canna know how happy we be, and how bad I be wanten to see Jean. Does she know o' my comen?" Angus answered, "Nay, Freddy, she dinna know. It be to ye delight that ye surprise her. She ha' been waiten ye." Angus continued, "And Kenny, lad, I can tell ye Heather has too been waiten. She and Jean ha' become good friends and Jean be tellen her if ye want somethen bad enough it could happen, and she be a wanten and wanten real bad. I hope that make ye happy." Ken said, "Thanks, Angus, it does."

Since we left Auralee, three months had past by our time, but here only eighteen days had gone by. Even if we did return, the girls would have been expecting a longer wait. I looked at Ken and said, "Well, ole buddy, I pretty much know what to say, how about you?" He squirmed, twisted, and said, "Oh, I'll know, I'll know."

I told Angus we wanted to keep America and Illinois and wondered where we would live. He replied, "Aye, lads, ye may keep ye ponies, and donna ye worry; all things will be cared for in time." I thought, *Truly hope so, I only know we are one heck of a far piece from Chicago.*

CHAPTER 13

A FAR PIECE FROM CHICAGO

Anxiously I said to Angus, "Sir, I wish to see Jean as soon as possible and Ken wants to see Heather." He took a long puff on his pipe, smiled broadly, and said, "Aye, lads, Jean be at home and Heather is at her croft nearby. She lives alone with her sheep dog, Candy, and raises a herd o' sheep. Her parents both passed on a couple o' years ago, lost them to an unknown malady. I willa tell ye, Kenny, on how ye go there, it na' be far."

From the bridge we hurried as fast as Angus's cart and the ponies could take us and on the way Angus mentioned we had only been away from Auralee for eighteen days. "Ye surprised me ye returnen this soon." Ken replied, "Yes, Sir, it surprised us too, but many things pointed to our being able to come back; thus, we were determined to get here."

Ken's quick response interested me. Suddenly he was championing our journey and that pleased me. We soon arrived and Auralee looked the same as she did when we were here three months ago by Chicago time. It was still early morning, the roosters were crowing, the cows were mooing, and a few people were hustling about seeing to their morning chores. Everything had very much a storybook appearance; my good first impressions of Auralee certainly were still in place. On our way, Angus told us, "For a few days, the both of ye will be sharing Mary's old room. She and her husband, John Gregory, be married a few days after ye left. It was a joyous occasion, only saddened a wee bit by ye leaven. But ye nay fret, lads, ye be back and be that wha' matters." Angus continued, "Freddy, lad, we be nearly to my house and I leave ye to surprise Jean. I willa go wi' Kenny to show him the way to Heather's home." I thanked Angus and began to gather my courage. Ken said, "Good luck, ole buddy, see you soon." I managed a smile, waved, and turned toward Jean's home.

****

As I neared, Jean was outside working in her garden, weeding the little plants. My reaction was, *how like her.* She had her back to me and did not notice my approach…. About ten feet away I said softly, *"I love you, Jean."* She stopped, straightened up, and slowly turned. Her expression was one of clear shock. She stood motionless for some time, as did I.

Then she spoke, "Freddy, oh, Freddy, it be really you?" I said, "Aye, bonnie Jean, it is me, and I'm here to stay with you." By now tears were streaming down her lovely cheeks, and she rushed into my open arms. We were both so full of feeling and emotion; we kissed passionately.

"Oh, Freddy, my prayers, my prayers, they be answered. I be forever so happy. Tell me again that ye truly be here for me." "Yes, Jean, I am here if you will have me." She answered, "Aye, Freddy ye canna' know how very much I be prayen for this day. Come ye, we must be finden Angus." I said, "He knows and is taking Ken, who has also returned, to see Heather. Angus told us she has been hoping for his return." Jean laughed, "Aye, Freddy, that is true. I be so excited, it be as though we will all live forever."

****

Meanwhile Angus and Ken walked to Heather's home. Her dog, Candy, was first to notice their approach and responded as any faithful watchdog would do, with a lot of barking. Angus waved his arm, Candy recognized him, and stopped barking. Angus said, "Kenny, I be leaven ye here now. Heather willa nay be far away. Ye and Freddy be now on ye own, but know today thee have made this old man very happy."

I looked about and did not see any evidence of Heather but reasoned Cindy would know where to find her. So I yelled, "Go, Cindy, go find Heather," and waved my hand outward. She took off running down a little path toward a small wooded area behind her croft (farm) and I followed. Her flock was bleating and milling nearby; *I believe I sorta like these little guys.*

Suddenly there she was, shawl around her shoulders, standing in a field full of beautiful purple clover and talking softly to her flock. "Git away laddy, whoa, girl, and so forth." Momentarily I stood and just watched her as a little honey bee whizzed by me. She was so gentle with her sheep and beautiful as I remembered her. Finally I softly said, *"Heather, Heather, I am here."* She slowly turned and the look on her face was priceless. Surprise, shock, as understanding had not yet sunk in.

I continued, "Heather, it is me, Kenny, and I have returned to Auralee to be with you. Please come to me." Heather was still a little dumbfounded, but she walked slowly toward me. I held out my hand and as she neared she took it and said, "Kenny, you be such a handsome man. Are my prayers truly answered? You coom here for me?" "Heather, yes, if you give me a chance." "Aye, Kenny, I give ye a chance," and she threw her arms about me and gave me a great big kiss. I thought, *Well, I guess that is answer enough.*

I continued, "Heather, let's sit down and talk, there is much to tell you. First, Freddy is also here and is with Jean. He and I will be staying for a time in Mary's old room at Angus's home. When you are ready we will go see them."

Heather replied, "I be so grateful ye ha' come back," threw her arms about me again and we kissed and kissed. She had definitely recovered from her surprise and shock. She continued, "I be in love wi' ye, Kenny, since the first we met at the festival. Ye ha' at all times been wi' me in my mind. I be so thankful." We kissed again and I thought to myself, *Think this is going to work out fine,* and said, "Let's go find Fred and Jean." She smiled warmly, "Aye, that we must do." We got up and started our walk to Angus's home. Cindy was left to mind the flock; she understood her role well.

****

When Ken and Heather arrived, I waved, said, "Hey, you guys, the gangs all here." Then I realized Heather and Jean probably didn't have the foggiest idea of what that meant. I hurried to say, "Glad we are all together once more." Heather ran to Jean and threw her arms around her and hugged her tightly. They both were giggling like two little children who had just eaten some forbidden candy. Jean said, "Aye, Heather and I are so blessed this day for our wishes and prayers ha' been answered. We must go now to see Reverend Dundee and thank him."

Angus who just joined us said, "Aye, lads and lassies, we be owing him a visit as Freddy's and Kenny's first obligation to their pledge o' now becomen citizens o' Auralee forever. Dinna ever ye forget ye are a citizen of Auralee and her time. Ye no longer be Americans, and thee twenty-first century is speeding away on her own journey."

I replied, "Aye, Angus, Ken and I pledge that we have made our choice. We are happy to become citizens of Glen Auralee and will always keep the faith. We will cherish our past time and it will live on in our memories. Ken and I have only one important request to make, and it best wait until we talk with Reverend Dundee." Angus added, "Aye, Freddy, now let us be on our way. He be expecten us."

We left on what would be less than a fifteen minute walk. I held Jean's hand and Ken held Heather's. We didn't say too much, just too excited, I guess. When we arrived, Reverend Dundee was on his porch, smoking his pipe just as he had been when we first visited with him. As we approached, he arose and said, "Aye, Freddy and Kenny, welcome ye back to Auralee. Please be siten here wi' me." We took our seats in a circle of chairs he arranged for us.

****

Angus spoke first, "Reverend Dundee, Freddy and Kenny ha' taken the pledge o' becomen citizens o' Glen Auralee wi' all it's covenants, and ye know o' their interests in Jean and Heather. Freddy ha' a question or favor to ask o' ye."

Reverend Dundee deliberated for a time, took several drags on his pipe allowing the smoke to curl toward the heavens in small ringlets, then spoke. "Freddy and Kenny, lads, ye be now citizens o' Glen Auralee, and ye be welcome. Ye will come to realize, as your Elder, I wi' always be here for thee. But I be not one to try to govern everythen. I be here for advice and counsel. Now, Freddy, what be your question or favor?"

I felt very pressed. *I better get my question framed right the first time.* I began, "Reverend Dundee, I will try to make my request brief. Ken and I come from a place some 250 years in the future. During those years there have been great developments made in all fields of endeavor. In many, such as medicine and education, the improvements have been vast. In a limited way, we feel we can bring considerable comfort to the sick, and bring you some new ideas in the areas of medicine and teaching.

"It will never be our objective to change things in Auralee just to be more like where we came from. We are here because we love what life is like in Auralee. Reverend Dundee, we nay want to change her, only make her better and our fellow citizens happier. Those will be Ken and my goals.

"In keeping with these objectives, we are asking that Ken and myself be permitted to visit Penoaken in our old time upon occasion to re-supply ourselves with medicines and items which would benefit all living in Glen Auralee. I suggest our trips last no longer than one day, Auralee time (five days Penoaken time), and we return there no more often than each 4 to 6 months Auralee time. Thank you, Sir, for listening."

Once more the good Reverend went into a contemplative huddle with himself. It took him a good five minutes before he replied, and meanwhile none of us said a thing. I mean it was really quiet. At last, Reverend Dundee removed the pipe from his mouth, laid in on the table, and said. "Aye, Freddy, ye ask me a question and I believe everything ye say is made wi' only good intent in ye mind.

"I nay be certain I can grant ye permission to leave and return to Auralee no matter how good ye intentions be. Give me some time. I will go to where I contemplate on great matters, and consult wi' God, if he be o' listenen. Go now, and I will ask ye to return when I have an answer." I said, "Thank you, Sir, and good luck."

He arose, picked up his pipe and in studied concentration went inside his house to be alone with his thoughts. Ken, Angus, Heather, Jean, and I silently returned to Angus's home. It was time to officially begin our lives in Auralee and await Reverend Dundee's reply.

****

Ken left with Heather for her home and Jean and I went to the square where we sat on a bench near the fountain under a giant tree. It was quiet and this afforded us time to once more chat. The birds were singing, the air was still, pleasantly warm, and sunny. Jean said, "Freddy, I be so happy and my mind be all in a dither, I dinna' want this day to ever end. Please tell me why ye came back to Auralee. I want to hear it from ye own self."

I smiled, gave her a small kiss on the cheek and began. "Jean, look here." I removed from my pocket the little silver ring she had placed on my finger when I left on my return trip back to 2008. "This little ring was never far from me and it served as a constant memory of you. There was never any doubt in my mind that I had fallen in love with you, but our very different worlds and lifestyles gave me concerns for your continued happiness and they were paramount in my decision to leave Auralee.

"After returning home both Ken and I had ample opportunities to reconsider our decisions. We were not happy with our present lives, felt we would be better off in your world, and wished to be with the girls we knew we could forever love and who we believed loved us too. As in your dream, we had several signs which indicated our return was desired and possible. So, Jean, Ken and I decided to take a chance and place our futures in the hand of your little ring. You had told me that if I was ever in need, this ring would bring me to you, and here we are."

Jean looked at me, smiled that delightful smile, and replied, "Aye, Freddy, my dearest, what a delightful story. I willa cherish ye tellen it to me and never, never ye worry for one moment about me forgetten it or of my love for thee."

I said, "Thank you, Jean. For the rest of the afternoon could we walk about Auralee and the nearby countryside? I wish to begin my familiarization education. Please show me anything and everything. Then one day soon you can take me to Nevis and Dee for the same purpose. Both Ken and myself want to become beneficial citizens of your Glen Auralee." Jean continued, "Freddy, I nay be surprised at ye request. For ye and Kenny to be anything else than good citizens, that would be my surprise. Give me ye hand and we be on our way."

****

We left Jean's home and for the next two hours we walked the streets of Auralee past the square, the fountain, and the school which also served as the village church. She told me how she instructed the children in both instances. We visited the bakery where bread, pies, and other goodies were baked. The aroma was very pleasant and I was able to sample some of the products.

Finally we stopped at a small park on the banks of the Norr Sea. It was a pleasant place and an inspiring thought crossed my mind, *This would be an ideal place for a par three golf course, club house, practice green, and driving range...gotta think long range.* After about a half hour talking about the birds and flowers we returned to Jean's home. By now it was 4:40 PM and time for supper. Ken and Heather had already arrived, and some of the neighbor ladies had prepared a fine meal of fried chicken, fresh mixed vegetables, and potato pudding. It was great, just like grandma used to make. I thought, *You know this did taste much the same as mom's cooking too.* It was amazingly delightful.

After dinner Ken, Angus, and myself assigned America and Illinois "quarters" for the duration of their stay in Angus's corral. They seemed to be comfortable with their new home and hungrily munched away on their fodder. Ken and I were glad to see them accept it.

Later that first evening we all talked about our request to Reverend Dundee that we be permitted to travel back-and-forth between here and Penoaken. Angus said, "Nay ye worry, lads, the good Reverend willa do for ye all that canna be done."

We thanked him; it wasn't long before Ken walked Heather home, soon returned, and went to bed. Jean and I went outdoors for a few minutes; the evening was very bright and delightfully cool. I took her in my arms and kissed her once, then twice, then thrice, and said "Jean, I love you, and revel in the thought that we shall have a lifetime to be together."

She smiled and spoke, "Aye, Freddy, we shall, and be this a proposal?" I chuckled, "No, Jean, not yet. When I do propose it will be a little more formal and will be after I ask Angus for your hand." She replied, "Aye, Freddy, that be as it should. I willa wait for as long as ye wish and cherish the thought that it willa be. I be very happy now." We then reentered the house. Ken, already in bed, was snoring lightly and I soon joined him.

****

The next morning after breakfast Ken returned to visit Heather. Jean and I began our trip to the small village of Dee, located 4 miles to the northeast of Auralee with a population of about 200. This would be an exciting experience. My first ride in one of the quaint little carts that most families seemed to have, comparable to the family car, I supposed. They were drawn by a single Shetland pony. These were magnificent little horses, about one third the size of a normal horse, but they were very hardy and strong animals. They pulled all sorts of apparatus from plows to the family cart.

Our trip to Dee took about an hour and along the way Jean pointed out features of Glen Auralee. We passed wooded areas, fields of clover, and several crofts (farmhouses). She told me who lived in each of them, but that was a bit much for me to assimilate on my first day.

It was lovely countryside covered with trees, grasses, and hills abounding with heather. We passed pastures with herds of cattle and sheep. The cows were considerably different in appearance from what I was used to, rather long horns with a coat which looked somewhat like it was borrowed from a buffalo. In either case, the omnipresent Scottish Sheepdog was barking and herding it's way from one end of the pasture to the other. They were friendly little rascals and extremely efficient at their jobs.

We passed several more crofts, arrived at Dee around eight o'clock, and were welcomed by Mayor Osmas Frazier. Sporting his finest kilts, he stood at a hardy 5'5", graying hair, about 50 years old, long beard and a full mustache. There was no doubt where we were. I said to myself, *Aye, laddy, ye be in ole Scotland afore ye.* Jean said, "Good morning, Mayor Frazier, this be Freddy Mitchell, a new citizen o' our bonnie Glen." Mayor Frazier smiled and removed his pipe, seemed everyone sported one. I considered maybe I should get one. The Mayor said, "Aye, Freddy Mitchell it be? Ye be the first outsider to be welcomed to our land and ye be most welcome, Sir."

I answered, "Thank you most sincerely, Mayor Frazier, I am honored." He boarded our "auto-cart" and stood behind Jean and myself; there was seating for only two. He began his narration, "Mind ye, laddy, Dee be a wee village, but it be a bonnie place." He continued, "Across the way be our village square with it's fountain where we obtain most o' our water which comes from both thee North River and thee East Creek. Our kirk (church) be just beyond it. When it na' be in service it be our place o' learnen. Over there be our bakery." He really didn't need to tell me as the aroma defined it.

We stopped, Mayor Frazier got off, and went into the bakery returning in a couple minutes with two large slabs of bread smothered with a sweet butter. We accepted his offering and I took a big bite. It was delightful, just the slightest bit grainy, but I could handle that.

We continued our tour for about four blocks until we arrived at the East Creek. To the north was a wooded area with several benches and tables spread out beneath the trees. Mayor Frazier explained this was where folks came to meditate and thank God for their deliverance, and where occasionally there were games and fishen contests.

I was surprised at how orderly and clean everything continued to be. It was obvious everyone took pride in their communities. We returned to the square. I thanked Mayor Frazier for the tour and told him I now understood why he was so proud of his community. Dee was truly a wee and bonnie place. As Jean and I said our goodbyes he said, "Do ye come back, lad, ye be always welcome." As we drove away the mayor waved his hat above his head.

We headed our cart northwesterly for about a mile where we crossed a bridge that spanned the North River to a small island which Jean called the Outland. She told me the island was populated by two crofter families, their sheep dogs, a few cats, a couple of cows, some chickens, and a large herd of sheep. The scenery was spectacular with small pristine munros along the north coast and open meadows to the south. Jean said it be a lonely life, but a happy one. We drove about the island, stopping to say hello to members of the Harold and Carne families. They were very cordial and seemed pleased we visited their small world.

From there we "sped" back to Auralee. It was now 3:00 PM and time for Jean to pitch in with preparing our evening meal. Ken had spent his day learning the life of a sheep herder...and who knows what else. He didn't arrive until 4:30. I really didn't trust anything those two might do. I offered, "Good day, Ken?" He grinned rather sheepishly and I replied, "Yeh."

For the remainder of the evening we chatted. I wanted to talk about my intentions with Jean and where we might live in the future. Then, there was Ken. Gotta think about him too. I realized it was too early to bring these things up, but not too early to be thinking about them. At 8:30 Ken walked Heather home and when he returned we retired.

****

Morning arrived, my third day as a citizen of Auralee. Mary, Jean's sister, had arrived earlier to help with breakfast which consisted of: lamb chops, homemade bread with butter and apple jam, a strong cheese similar to limburger, and fresh milk. Noticeably missing was coffee and Angus was quick to add, "We na have coffee nor tea often as thee be in very short supply, only on special occasions." It was fine with us as fortunately we were not hooked on them.

After breakfast Jean and I proceeded to the corral to prepare for our visit to Nevis and Ken left for Heather's place. America and Illinois were wagging their tails as if they expected me to take them along, but once again it was Jean's pony, Patience, who got the call. Jean's other two pets were on hand to give us their send-off. Her sheep dog, Lassie, and her cat, Kitty. I swear, *Everything in this place is cute and adorable.* We boarded our cart and again "sped off" on our 4 mile trip to Nevis.

Meanwhile Ken would tour the area around Heather's croft which was about 1 mile south of Jean's home. Heather's home stood alone, surrounded by trees and nestled among some low hills that were covered with heather and various other wild flowers. The pastures where her sheep grazed were extensive and the work of her dog Candy was impressive and imperative to their welfare. Fortunately there were no predators in Glen Auralee. Our 4 mile trip had taken us almost two hours via open pastures, some full of cattle, sheep, and past several crofts. It was almost ten o'clock when we arrived at Nevis. We had not hurried, we paused to enjoy the scenery, sneaked a kiss or two, or was it three? *Oh, well, who was counting?*

At the village square Jean introduced me to Mayor John McDougall. He was somewhat more than I had expected, 6 feet tall, blond. sparkling blue eyes, 200 pounds, and very Nordic in appearance. As with Mayor Frazier he was resplendent in his tartan and a large pendent announcing his office was prominently displayed on his sash.

The mayor was accompanied by a four piece bagpipe band and several of the locals. The band, three pipes and a snare drum, were bleating a tune that Jean informed me was *Bonnie Auralee.*

Mayor McDougall offered me his hand and as I stepped down from my cart, he said, "Welcome ye, Freddy Mitchell, to our village o' Nevis. It be my pleasure to take ye on a tour o' our town. Do ye ha' anything specific ye wish to see?" I replied, "No, Sir, nothing special. Just an overall tour will do fine." He smiled, we boarded our cart, and to the tune of *Bonnie Auralee* departed. We passed through the square and meandered through a residential area. As in Dee things were orderly, neat, and many people were standing along the streets waving to welcome us.

Finally we arrived at the shore of Loch Norr. Mayor McDougall stopped at the wharf and fish market. As we entered the area we could tell by the odor that fish products were involved. It wasn't too strong and the Mayor pointed out that the winds ordinarily carried the odor out to sea. It was here that they got their saltwater foods. Their fresh water fishing took place at both the Easterly Creek and North River areas.

The residue from preparing the fish for consumption was taken by small boats and dumped several hundred yards off shore where the tides flushed the remains out to sea. Several varieties of seabirds were in abundance to scavenge anything left over. The freshly cleaned fish were next transported by cart or boat to Auralee and Dee where they were always consumed within 36 hours. I found this very interesting.

From there we passed a wooded park and the bakery; of course, it was sample time, a slice of warm apple tart covered with sweet butter. It was apparent cholesterol and blood sugar wasn't high on the local's priority lists. I'd have to keep up my exercise regime.

Jean had remained very quiet during our tour and left the talking up to me and the Mayor. We finished the tour by noon and politely turned down the Mayor's offer for lunch, saying we had an appointment back in Auralee. We thanked him profusely and promised we would spend more time in Nevis.

On the way back to Auralee we passed through more pastures well stocked with cattle and sheep. Small hills covered with heather and wooded areas abounded. As the road passed near Heather's place we decided to surprise her and Ken with a visit. As we neared, in the distance we could see Heather's flock with Candy roaming about them. Ken and Heather were not in sight. I told Jean we had better approach with discreet caution and she laughed, saying, "Aye, Freddy, ye be right. Best we do that. We shall sing *Bonnie Auralee* so they canna miss our comen." I said, "Good thinking, Jean, and before we get there, I have something for you."

I pulled her to my side and planted a great big kiss on her lips saying, "Jean, bonnie Jean, with every passing day, I love you more." She smiled that delightful little smile and said, "Ay, Freddy, and I love thee in the same way. I be ready for ye to talk with my father whenever ye be." My reply was, "Soon, Jean, soon." Jean began singing and I joined in. We made enough racket to get Candy's attention and hoped we had done the same for Heather and Ken.

****

As we approached, we first saw Heather merging from the chicken house near the shelter at the sheep coral. She had a basket on her arm and had apparently been collecting eggs. At the same time Ken emerged from the front door of the house. Apparently all was normal, no surprises here today. They both waved, we stopped our singing and hollered, "Hello there."

We tied up our cartmobile, stepped down and asked "What be happenen?" Ken replied, "Hey you world travelers, we've been well occupied. I have been telling Heather of my plans to get involved with teaching, along with helping her here at the croft." Jean spoke first, "Oh, Kenny, that be so wonderful. Perhaps I canna be o' some help to ye. Teachen be one o' my favorite pastimes."

Ken was quick to respond asking Jean to suggest any of her friends who might be qualified to teach. He continued, "I will set up an instructors course for them and we will make the job into more just an occasional pastime. I'll need the help of dedicated folks. We'll make it fun, but it must be done in a professional manner." Jean responded, "Aye, Kenny, I understand ye, and do have in my mind a few folk." After a half hour of talking, Jean and I left for home. Ken said he would follow soon and Heather would remain, alone, just her, Candy, her chickens, and sheep.

****

Last night Ken had told me Heather understood our situation, but he was getting tired of leaving her and hoped we could move ahead with plans that would include her and Jean in them. I agreed, and said, "Ken, I intend tomorrow to open the subject of my intentions with Jean, and of our moving to more permanent quarters as soon as possible." He replied, "Swell, Fred, and you may as well know, for planning purposes, I intend to marry that lass. Don't know how it may work out but, as they phrase it here, I be beginen to ha' a real liken for her." I answered, "Great, Ken. Think you will make a fine couple. You, Heather, Candy, the chickens, and the sheep. But at least you won't be planting seeds." We both laughed heartily.

****

Dinner was at 5:00 PM and afterwards we men retired to the sitting room. Angus lit his pipe, and when he appeared relaxed and comfortable, I said, "Angus, I have a couple of serious subjects to talk with you about. The first one deals with where and when will Ken and I be moving from your lovely home to one of our own. Perhaps Ken may be able to answer for himself, but the second deals with what I do in the near future. Therefore, Angus, I would be pleasured if now you would accompany me to a more private sanctuary, say to the church." Angus continued to puff on his pipe for awhile, then grinned, said, "Freddy, lad, it be my honor to accompany ye to thee kirk." During the short walk to the church no words passed between us until after we had entered and taken a seat in a pew near the alter. I spoke first.

"Angus, Sir, I suppose it is no surprise to you that I love Jean very much. Therefore, I am asking you for permission to marry her as soon as I am settled in a manner which will permit me to provide for her in a home of our own. That brings me to the second question. How, Sir, do I acquire property and how do I go about building a home on it?" Angus laughed as a cloud of smoke from his pipe swirled toward the ceiling, "Aye, Freddy they be fair and good questions. First o' all, lad, I nay be able to answer you in any manner other than it willa be my pleasure to welcome thee into my family. Jean be very much in love with ye. She ha' been waiten for these years and ye be her man." I took a deep breath and thanked Angus for his best wishes.

"Now, Sir, please don't say anything to Jean. I want to await the most proper time to ask her." Of course Angus agreed. He continued, "Now, laddy, regarding the second question. It also be an easy answer. Four years ago I had work started on a new home to be occupied by Jean and her future. I be sure that her dreams and hopes would someday come true and now they ha'. Come ye with me and I will show ye thee place."

As we walked south past a small wooded area we came to a place south of Auralee not far from Heather's croft. Set back a short distance from the road, ground had been cleared, a cellar dug, sturdy foundations in place, and timbers lay stacked ready for use. Angus said, "Here it be, Freddy. There be plenty o' space for a nice house, gardens, stable, and corral." I was dumbfounded. I had passed this place before, but never dreamed it would be my future home. I turned to Angus, "What a lovely place this is. How soon will it be ready?" Angus chuckled, "As soon as ye be ready wi' your plans we get started. There be plenty o' folk to help ye." I replied, "We'll get started soon, don't know how to thank you." Again he smiled, "Aye, Freddy, we be happy to do it. It be a fun time and a pleasure to us."

CHAPTER 14

A TIME FOR YOU AND ME

I was beginning to feel as if Auralee was truly my home and mentioned this to Ken. He admitted that contrary to his earlier premonitions, he too was starting to settle in. Heather, he said, was making a profound difference. She was totally a different person from what he had originally thought, responsible for and dedicated to her flock, as opposed to being frivolous.

I said, "Ken, here's an idea. Let's propose to Heather and Jean at the same time and make it a double wedding. I feel certain the girls will be happy with that. What do you think?" He replied, "Good idea, ole buddy. You know I had been thinking the same thing. When do we do this?" I replied, "Are you ready?" Ken answered, "Yep. How about proposing tomorrow?" I quickly said, "You're on. Tomorrow there will be a festival at the village square. We'll do it separately, but at the same time. We'll meet you and Heather at ten o'clock, then each of us will go our own way, and later get back together." Ken replied, "Sounds great to me. Let's have a go at it."

Saturday morning was a nice day, partly cloudy but only a slight breeze and the temperature highs would probably be in the mid-sixties. At ten o'clock the four of us arrived at the festival and picked a seat near the fountain. Festivities were underway, the ladies setting up the tables and booths for food service. After a few minutes Ken said, "I have something I want to discuss with Heather. We'll see you back here in an hour or so." I answered, "OK," then turned to Jean and said, "that sounds like a good idea, let's go for a walk too." She quickly agreed and the four of us departed. Ken and Heather proceeded east while Jean and I went south to the little wooded area we had visited on my first visit to Auralee.

****

After a few minutes of talking with her little friends, the birds, I took Jean's hand, pulled her to my side, kissed her lovingly and said, "Jean, I love you dearly. Since returning to Auralee each time we are together you make me feel I am more than I can be…. Will you marry me?"

Jean's eyes twinkled like Fourth of July sparklers, her face broke into one of her finest smiles, and tears began rolling down her beautiful cheeks. After a few moments she said, "Aye, Freddy. I willa marry ye. Thee canna know how happy this makes me feel. It be all my dreams come true." She threw her arms once again about me and we kissed and kissed for about the next five minutes.

Finally when we came up for some much needed air I continued, "Jean, I am so happy and now for some more good news. First, I have talked with your father and he has given us his full blessing. Second, at this very time Ken is proposing to Heather. Third, Ken and I want to make this a double wedding if you and Heather agree."

Jean spoke without delay, "Aye, Freddy, ye ha' my agreement and I be certain Heather will be accepten too." I added, "It's settled then; we will set the date later. Come on now, let's hurry back to the festival."

When we arrived Ken and Heather were waiting for us. Ken had proposed to Heather; she was ecstatic and delighted over the prospect of a double wedding. As the girls saw each other they rushed into each others arms. They were so happy, jumping around, and laughing like two bonnie little children.

It was apparent to everyone what had happened, but they were discreet and left the tellen for Jean and Heather to delight on. The four of us mingled among the visitors. The festivals were always well attended, and I guessed today's attendance to be in excess of 600.

Most people at the festival were involved playing games such as lawn bowling, races, dancing, and storytelling. At 1:00 PM Mayor Bright had the pipers herald a town meeting. When everyone had assembled at the fountain, Mayor Bright spoke. "Welcome folk o' Glen Auralee. Jean Macgregor and Heather Crawford ha' a special somethen to tell ye."

All smiles, Jean and Heather joined Mayor Bright and Heather said, "It be me pleasure to tell ye that Kenny Effington ha' asked me to marry and Freddy Mitchell ha' asked Jean to wed. It will be a double wedden and the date willa be set soon…an occasion for a special festival."

Everyone broke into a loud cheer and called for us to say something. It appeared I was the chosen spokesman. As the drummers gave me a big drum roll, I stepped up on an elevated area at the fountain and began, "Our dear friends of Glen Auralee, the four of us thank you from the bottom of our hearts for your gracious best wishes.

"We expect the date to be mid October and hope to see you all at the wedding, which we hope can be held here at the square. Thank you all again." I waved Ken, Jean, and Heather to stand beside me; as they did there was more clapping and hollering while the band played *Bonnie Auralee*. After the emotions had somewhat ebbed the four of us ate a fine lunch, said our so-longs, and headed back to our respective abodes.

****

The next week Ken and I asked Angus to meet with us regarding where we might go on our honeymoons; also, Jean and I wanted to talk with him about starting on our new home. What Ken and Heather's plans might be, I was not sure?

Angus was delighted to be included in our plans and the four of us decided on the following Tuesday morning for our meeting. Over the weekend we decided on the second Saturday in October for the weddings. Jean and I discussed various ideas for our new home and Ken told us that for the time being he would make some additions to Heather's place and reside there. Finally we agreed to ask Reverend Dundee, the Elder, to perform our double ceremony.

Tuesday morning arrived and the four of us were very excited about our meeting with Angus. At breakfast an unexpected treat awaited us, *Coffee.* The aroma was great and reminded us of our recent past. We drank it black; it was a bit strong, but we managed.

Angus began to describe our wedding retreats. There weren't many choices. He offered us two locations. One was across the channel in the mountains northeast of Auralee along the Norr Sea coast. The other in the hills east of Nevis near the East Creek. Both were secluded and had lovely views. Ken and I drew for first choice and I won. After talking to Jean, I chose the place on the Norr Sea.

****

During the next few weeks Jean and Heather kept busy readying their wedding dresses, continuing their daily work, and gossiping eagerly amongst their girl friends. Ken and I were busy getting work started on our respective abodes. Angus maintained his status as foreman on both projects and soon there was a veritable army of workers, young and old, working diligently on our projects whose completions were expected by October 1st.

Some of the work was fortunately already complete on Jean's and my place. The cellar was dug, foundations were in place, rafters had been cut, and a large fireplace was under construction. Ken had decided to add a room to Heather's one room croft which now served her as a kitchen, living area, and bedroom. The new room would double the space available and serve primarily as a bedroom with ample storage closets. It was a sizeable task but Angus said, "Now dinna ye worry, lads. This be a merry time for we folk. A pleasure to make ye welcome and happy in Auralee." I turned to Ken, "This ain't Chicago." He answered, "Nope."

The first half of September was a busy time for all of us. Ken and I had two very important meetings on tap. One with Reverend Dundee was scheduled for the 5th to hear his report on our request to be able to occasionally transit between Auralee and Penoaken (twenty-first century). The second meeting on the 10th was to inform the Mayors of Auralee, Nevis, and Dee regarding some programs we hoped to initiate. Ken and I spent most of our time when not overseeing our new homes discussing these two major upcoming events.

Often when Ken and I had some free time we would go to some secluded place and just talk. On one occasion we found ourselves reminiscing about Chicago and the folks back there. Ken said, "You know, Fred, I am going to be happy here with Heather, but I still catch myself thinking about the good times we had back home. Do you miss them." I answered, ""Yeh, I still do, but right now I am just too busy. That's something I can think about later." He responded with his usual brevity, "Yeh, I suppose so."

****

On September 5th, Ken, Angus, and myself appeared at Reverend Dundee's home at 9:00 AM. It was time to find out the most important piece of information we would ever encounter. So many things depended upon what he might tell us. I was anxious as was Ken. Angus appeared calm, cool, and collected as though he did not have a worry in the world. For better or for worse we stood ready.

Revered Dundee greeted us with, "Angus, lads, I know ye be ready to hear from me as to ye request ye be able to travel occasionally back to Penoaken and return to Glen Auralee. I canna keep ye waiten any longer.... *It be possible ye be able to do that.* There be a few conditions and I willa tell ye o' them." Ken's and my face lit up like we had just been delivered our own miracle. We wanted to cheer, but waited for more details in constrained silence.

Reverend Dundee continued, "Gentlemen, ye be able to make a trip no more often than every four months, Auralee time (20 months Penoaken time) and ye canna stay away longer than 24 hours Auralee time (5 days Penoaken time). Ye canna return to Glen Auralee wi' any persons or items beyond those you will be usen in your professions without specific approval, as we dinna wish to be in any manner a part o' that world."

Ken and I looked at each other. At last I spoke, "Sir, we are quite happy with this decision. We appreciate the seriousness of our leaving Auralee and returning. Sir, we shall never violate the provisions you have presented to us. Do you agree, Ken?" He answered unhesitantly, "Yes, I do concur." Reverend Dundee concluded, "Then it be done. Angus, you willa be in charge o' the lad's travels." He responded it would be his pleasure.

That evening Ken and I separately explained this decision to Heather and Jean. They were surprised and wanted to know more, but we told them details would unfold as we came closer to a visit. It the meantime we had many more important things to do in the near term like prepare ourselves for our upcoming meeting with the mayors.

****

On the 10th Ken, Angus, Reverend Dundee, and I attended the meeting with Mayors Bright, MacDougal, and Frazier of Auralee, Nevis, and Dee respectively. It was now Ken and my first attempt at explaining some of our plans for supplementing Glen Auralee's educational and medical provisions (both were lacking any professional basis). Ken was up first and after a brief introduction he began:

"Sirs, it is my pleasure that I am able to present you with a plan which I believe can greatly improve education in Auralee. Please permit me to tell you I am very impressed with the ongoing work your present volunteers are doing.

"What I am proposing is a system that can bring to your young people techniques which have been developed over the last 250 years of our old earth time. Fred and I spent countless hours designing the programs, we have brought with us a few teaching aides, and more can be added as Fred and I visit Penoaken. Essentially my plan will include children ages 6 through 15 consisting of several stages:

"Stage one: Interview and select a volunteer staff and train them on the new techniques, and select a site and equip it for classroom activities.

"Stage two: Pretest existing children for grade level capability.

"Stage three: Begin with classes grouped by age: ages 6-8, 1st thru 3rd grades, ages 9-11, 4th thru 6th grades, ages 12-14, 7th thru 9th grades, ages 15 plus, upper schooling.

"Stage four: Later I propose to institute schooling for those who have excelled in their studies. It would include intensive studies in such areas as: medicine, health, teaching, farming, and so on.

"This is a large undertaking and it will need a lot of help and support, With your approval, we will get started and details will evolve as we go. Now it is Fred's turn, here he is."

I took the stage, said, "Hello everybody, and thanks, Ken. You did a great job and I feel confident Glen Auralee will benefit greatly in the area of education. I only hope I can do as well.

"My offering comes in the area of medicine and hygiene. Taking advantage of my schooling in twenty-first century medical procedures, along with the use of some twenty-first century commonly available medicines, I will establish a medical clinic. I am not a surgeon nor a miracle worker. Yet I can be of great help to the citizens of Glen Auralee, making their lives healthier and caring for those emergency situations for which I am trained. This will require a facility from which to work and I will need a small trained staff to assist me.

"As a final note to push our plans forward, Ken and I would greatly appreciate your choosing a spokesperson to co-ordinate your questions, suggestions, and locations to be utilized. Ken and I will make ourselves available. Thank you for your attention."

It didn't take the committee long before Reverend Dundee had asked Mayor Bright and Angus to work with us and they readily agreed. Further the committee agreed that our proposals had extraordinary merit and assured us the entire Glen of Glen Auralee would add their support. It was music to our ears.

****

During the next few weeks until wedding bell time, Ken and I were well occupied working with the committee and establishing school and medical facilities. We established Auralee as the main location for both operations, and transportation by cart would be established between Nevis and Dee.

Additionally we were overseeing the construction of our homes where Jean and Heather had everything very much under control. In addition to this the girls had weddings to prepare for. Here they had lots of help. Mary and all their girl friends were interested and helpful. Everything was underway, food, drink, entertainment, and facilities.

This was one of the major benefits of life in Auralee. There was always plenty of volunteer help and everything was done as fun. No bickering about wages, time off, or who was in charge. Just pitch in, get the job done, and along the way enjoy yourself. It was a wonderful experience and Ken and I were rapidly growing accustom to life here.

Yet it was not to say that we never thought about our past lives. We did. One evening after a long day of hard work and meetings, while sipping an ale or two, I asked Ken, "What do you miss most of our old lives? About Chicago?"

He leaned back, thought for a moment, said, "Fred, that's easy. I miss TV, the Cubs, Pizza, my computer, the country club on weekends, and your constant bickering with Samantha. That's what I miss most. How about you, ole chum? By the way, I haven't forgotten that someday Pizza shall come to Auralee."

I laughed and responded, "Guess I miss much the same things, Ken, and I eagerly await for Pizza to arrive. Yet a few nights ago I had a vivid dream where my feelings about Chicago appeared before me. They were so clear that I grabbed a pencil, wrote them down, and memorized them. Listen to this:

"Asleep last night I saw the shadows of my past rush by me. Why did they go by so fast? When I awoke, now was the morrow laid before

me in this new land of mine as if, it seemed, I had unlimited time to borrow. But now I must look quickly for my morrow will soon be cast upon that hill already full of other shadows from my past. It is called inevitability, those mystic pictures passing so rapidly by me."

When I finished Ken sat for a moment then spoke. "Fred, that was really great. I enjoyed it. Sometimes I wish I could express myself as eloquently as you do." I answered, "Thanks for the kind words, but heck, you do just fine. Never, never change." He smiled, said, "OK, I won't"

The last two weeks before the wedding swiftly cascaded by. It was obvious Heather's croft would be ready in plenty of time. Although Angus assured us ours would be too, I had my fingers crossed. I took a few moments out and asked, "Bonnie Jean, are you a happy young lady?" There it was, that smile. I loved her more each time I saw it. "Aye, Freddy, I be happy. I be so happy I could cry with joy. We be happy, Freddy, the two o' us. My prophesy so sayeth."

****

The second Saturday in October, our wedding day, was suddenly and upon us. Fortunately everything seemed in order. Our homes were ready, the girls' dresses were ready, and the square was all set for our nuptials festival.

Ken and I were not permitted to see Jean and Heather from midnight on Thursday until the wedding on Saturday (an ole Scottish custom). Thus, we spent much of Friday with a few of our closest male friends at the festival tent which passed as the local pub. We called it, *The Pub,* in honor of it's namesake at the Travis Inn at Penoaken. On the other hand the girls spent their time at Jean and Angus's home chatting, laughing, sewing, eating, and giggling. Things seemed so simple when viewed from a twenty-first century perspective, so simple, so for real. We welcomed it.

The wedding was to begin Saturday morning at 10:00, and everyone was ready long before then. Jean and Heather were still fussing with their dresses and worrying about the flowers in their hair. America and Illinois were ready, majestically standing hitched to our honeymoon carts as if in eager anticipation of their upcoming journey.

Our carts were amply stocked for our three night stays at our honeymoon "lodges." For the grooms it was far simpler, we did nothing, just sat, smiled, and waited. At 10:00 Angus said in a loud authoritarian voice, "Coom ye lads and lassies. It be tyme." He marched with Jean, Heather and their attendants to the alter. John, (Mary's husband), Ken, our attendants, and I left by a slightly different route but ended at the same place. The Scottish pipes which had been piping *Bonnie Auralee* now changed to a tune quite akin to the Wedding March.

On the way I turned to Ken and said, "Are you nervous?" He looked at me and quipped, "Me, hell no, I'm not nervous, but never thought I would be doing this. Let alone not 250 years before I was born, in a world the size of a peanut, to a girl who maybe never was. Hell no, I am not scared, I am petrified." I laughed and said, "Ken, I am so happy and know you are too." He replied, "Yep, truth be known, let's get on with it." I answered, "Yep, let's do."

It seemed everyone in Glen Auralee was present, as though this was the big event of the year and I guessed it might just be. The trees, the fountain, and all the tents were festooned with flags and colorful banners. The wedding cakes were displayed in pinks and blues. Ken and I were very touched by all the expression of the friendship we saw around us. How different it was in Auralee… only sincere love for life and living.

Reverend Dundee was standing at the altar, bible in hand, and a huge smile covered his face. The Mayors of Auralee, Nevis, and Dee flanked him on his left and Angus and John stood to his right. For only a moment I sensed a very warm feeling, almost like crying. *But then…Crash!* Reality. I looked at Ken and he stared back, each of us with mouths agape and eyes rather squinted. *We looked at the girls.* Jean and Heather were smiling and appeared cool-as-a-cucumber. Obviously it didn't matter to them whether this was the twenty-first century or the eighteenth. We guessed some things never change.

Reverend Dundee began, "Ladies and gentlemen of Glen Auralee, now ye be here this morn to join two couples in holy matrimony, Jean Macgregor to Freddy Mitchell and Heather Crawford to Kenny Effington. Two different centuries be joined here today and nay let any man speak against it for this marriage be ordained by God, the Almighty." The crowd was very hushed.

Reverend Dundee continued, "Do ye Freddy Mitchell tak' Jean Macgregor as ye lawful wedded wife and do ye Kenny Effington tak' Heather Crawford as ye lawful wedded wife for all tyme until death do ye part? If ye do, then please answer, Aye." Ken and I looked at our brides and we answered, "I do, with love forever." Reverend Dundee smiled and closed his bible. "Aye pronounce ye be now man and wife. Ye can now kiss your brides." As we did the pipes were squealing something like *Here Comes the Bride.* I thought, *Taint everyone that can have a bagpipe band play at their wedding.*

We waved at the now cheering crowd and departed separately to our waiting carts which were decorated with all sorts of things. As we began to leave the square I was visited by one of my strange sensations, *Here I am, married to a girl who was born 250 years before me, leaving on my honeymoon on a cart pulled by a Scottish pony to a wedding retreat on a seacoast in a world about 30 square miles in size.* I shook my head and looked at Jean; she was so beautiful. I smiled and said, "Bonnie Jean, you are the meaning of my life. I have decided on this life and will never look back." She smiled and answered, "Ye be mine forever and ever."

****

Our trip took us less than a hour and when we arrived I was pleasantly surprised. It was a beautiful place, secluded and graciously surrounded by panoramic vistas of the sea, mountains, and of Glen Auralee. It was breathtaking and I said to Jean, "I love this place. Have you seen it before?" She responded, "Oh, nay, Freddy, I canna be here as it is a sacred place to be visited only once in their lifetime by new husbands and wives on their honeymoons." I nodded my head and thought to myself, *I am not surprised*.

I helped Jean down from the cart, took her hand and led her to the doorway of the house. At the threshold I picked her up in my arms, kissed her, and carried her inside. As I did I said, *"Bonnie Jean, my love, this is a tradition from my time,"* kissed her again and put her down. She said, "Oh, Freddy, tha' be so nice and ye can be doen it anytime ye like." Next we gathered our things from the cart, tethered America to a tree, and gave him his feed. He seemed to be entirely happy in his new world.

Jean and I took our belongings inside and as we had not eaten for some time we laid out a lunch of bread, cheese, wedding cake, and a robust tankard of heather ale. It wasn't much, but to both of us it tasted like the finest feast in the world. I think someone once said, *At a time like this, who cares about eating,* and if no one said it, I'll take credit for it.

****

After lunching Jean and I went outdoors to a grassy spot which overlooked the valley spread out before us. In the distance we could see the village of Auralee just across the North River. It was a splendid sight; the day was clear and warm. For a few minutes we talked of our plans for the future, plans for our home, my plans to establish a medical presence, and so forth.

Yet my heart and mind was elsewhere. I knew it was time that we prepare ourselves for a more physical presence to our marriage. I looked at Jean and she looked back at me. I could see desire written all over her face, she was breathing deeply and her eyes reflected anticipation. Quite likely my expression must have made a similar statement.

I held out my hand which she took. I pulled her close to my body and as we kissed she laid gently to the ground and my body snuggled down beside hers. I raised my head so that we could kiss and as we did I loosened her blouse which fell gently off her shoulders onto the ground exposing her heaving breasts. They were all I had anticipated. At the same time I loosened my shirt and it fell helplessly to my side. I cupped her breasts with my hands, passionately kissed her again and said, "Forever, my love."

I helped her disrobe as I myself did the same…we had now exposed all of our bodily features to each other and the experience was exhilarating. We were both breathing hard, about to intermesh ourselves in a ritual to consummate our marriage and our love for each other…as lovers have done since the origins of time.

After we had fulfilled our passion, we kissed once more and looked lovingly at each other. Words were not needed; our eyes bespoke feelings which were beyond mere expression. We calmly dressed and then hand in hand we quietly returned to the house and sat at a picnic table near the front door.

I said, "Jean, my love, from the first time I looked at you, you have been my heart, my soul." Tears rolled down her cheek as she softly replied, "Freddy, ye willa always be the man o' my dreams who I always knew would coom for me. There ne'er be any other."

The next two days sped by and all of a sudden it was time for our return to Auralee to begin our long lives together. During the last two days Jean and I had discussed having a family and we both wholeheartedly agreed we wanted children. She added we'd need to find out about Ken and Heather's plans. Jean was sure Heather would want a family. And I added, "Ken will too, in time, if not at first."

If there were things which Ken and I had learned since our arrival here, foremost among them was our world here is small and our population is limited. If we are to survive for long in this world we must remain in total support of each other at all times.

A big change from good old twenty-first century America. In Auralee money has no meaning. Only efforts expended by everyone on behalf of their fellow countrymen and their dedication to God's teachings have value. This does not mean we are all saints. On the contrary it means we work hard and believe in each others integrity. Reality here is pretty stark, but it is not to be feared, only admired and enjoyed.

CHAPTER 15

WORK TO BE DONE

FOR THE first week after returning from our weddings Ken, Heather, Jean, and I were very busy fending off well wishers. They were greatly appreciated and most came bearing a small gift; a cake, a candle, a handshake, a smile. We also talked about our honeymoons, although we respected each others privacy. We all agreed our "wedding resorts" were everything we had expected. Ken complained that there weren't any Pizza places to call, and we all chuckled at Ken being Ken.

The following week Ken and I thought it time to begin our efforts to set up our respective teaching and medical/hygiene facilities. We asked Angus to convene his committee of Mayors and Reverend Dundee. He agreed to do so, and the meeting was set for the next Thursday at the church.

Ken and I would spend the next days refining our plans. We had already involved Jean and Heather in putting together a list of would be candidates for positions such as teachers, teacher's aides, medical assistants, and nurses. Gender was not a consideration but being able to read, cipher, and write was necessary.

Jean and Heather presented Ken with a list of 10 folks they felt would be good teachers (7 women and 3 men). I was given a list of 6 prospects for medical/hygiene posts (3 men and 3 women). I noted two of the men were somewhat known for their work with animals. Didn't matter, we needed veterinarians too. We gathered all the information we could get on the prospects.

Thursday the committee gathered and we were once more on stage. Ken had honors and was first to speak. He began, "Good morning, gentlemen, I will be brief. As you will note, this is still a work in progress, but we need to start. My proposal is as follows:

"In order to conserve space and resources, such as teachers, combine ages 6-8, first, second, and third grades, ages 9-11, fourth, fifth, and sixth grades, ages 12-14, seventh, eighth, and ninth grades. Ages 15 and above will attend specialty classes.

"A list of teacher and medical candidates has been developed which includes 10 in the educational field and six in the medical.

"Now, gentlemen, before we can begin we need to select people, train them, create facilities to care for all students. We suggest all children be required to attend school through the 6th grade. Fred and I have brought with us an initial supply of teaching aids and medicines with which we can begin to use as soon as we have assistants trained. What we need now is space, places that can serve as schools and clinics. Gentlemen, so to speak, the ball is in your court. Thank you for your attention. Now, Fred, you're on."

I stood and began, "Thanks, Ken, for a great job and my part although just as important will be even briefer. I am also ready to begin serving Glen Auralee with medical and hygiene assistance. I have medicines with me and some medical knowledge that may well begin to improve health and well being of life in Auralee. I offer no magical cures, only better ways to avoid the dangers of infection and the emergency treatment of many injuries and maladies. I too am ready to begin service as soon as the same things Ken mentioned are attained. I thank you. Angus, it's yours."

Angus stood and said, "Lads, ye give a fine talk and ye be happy to know we be busy as well. We have spaces where ye can begin. The present school area at thee kirk can be added on to and we willa start work on that immediately. As for a medical facility, the kirk also has a couple o' small rooms for ye to use for now. We are to be builden facilities for ye both nearby and they be ready within 2 to 4 months. Ye and Kenny willa be providing supervision."

Reverend Dundee arose and said, "Freddy, Kenny, we bless thee and ye efforts. I canna wait for them to start." Everyone clapped and shook our hands. As we left I turned to Ken and summed it all up, "I am glad as all heck that this is over. Now the real work can begin." He replied, "Yep."

****

Next up was Saturday, festival time. At 9:00 AM Ken and I were invited to present to an expectant audience how or why it was we came to Glen Auralee. We considered this might be fun yet we could not take this opportunity lightly. Since Ken carried Thursday's meeting, I would get this one.

I talked over my presentation with Angus and he believed I would be best served to just tell my story in my own way. He said, "I be in no way wanten to spoil ye tale." Thus, without a hellava lot of advanced work, I should just show up and take on whatever came my way.

I showed up alright and was amazed at the number of folk gathered in and around the large tent put up for this meeting. I was surprised and flattered, or should I be scared? I considered, *Oh, well here goes.* I began:

"Ladies and gentlemen, let me offer you the following story and I sincerely hope it helps you with your understanding of why Ken and I decided to make Auralee our home and our lives.

"Last year by our time we visited Scotland for the purpose of grouse hunting. During our hunt we became lost and stayed the night in the woods. It was the night of May 14th, the night which Auralee became accessible from our world. Not knowing what was on the other side, we crossed the bridge and soon encountered Angus Macgregor who befriended us and led us for the next twelve hours on a visit of your world.

"I met Angus's daughter, Jean, and Kenny met Heather Crawford. It seems we were both smitten by the beauty and charm of these two maidens. We talked to Reverend Dundee and were offered the opportunity of staying in Auralee.

"We considered Reverend Dundee's offer at length and feared it would be difficult for us to adapt to a time which was 250 years behind our world. We also felt the girls would not be happy because of our differing views on life. Thus, our decision was to return to the twenty-first century.

"However, upon returning to our world, we experienced the same old routines and beliefs which had been bothering the both of us for a long time. We wished for a more simple life and came to realize Auralee offered us such a life.

"Later I began to experience dreams and had other indications which seemed to tell me perhaps we could return; thus, Ken and I set about making plans. Three months had passed by our time, but only 18 days had gone by here in Auralee.

"After returning to Scotland, we found our way back to the place we had first entered Auralee and waited. During the first night nothing happened and we despaired. We decided to wait another day and that evening we were rewarded by Auralee's reappearance. To our amazement Angus was there to greet us as we crossed the bridge. We had seriously pondered on our decision to return and told Angus we had come back determined to remain if you would have us. We were graciously accepted and you know the rest. We have no regrets. Thank you for taking us in."

Everyone stood, clapped, and cheered and we spent the next hour shaking hands. Jean and Heather stood next to us crying softly. Angus, Reverend Dundee, and the mayors of Auralee, Nevis, and Dee were all in attendance.

Reverend Dundee said, "Aye, Freddy, ye tell a fine story and know ye and Kenny be welcome here forever." We thanked him and I realized this day would be embedded in my psyche as the first real day of my life.

****

The next few days flew by; Ken and I continued to work with Jean and Heather on their candidate lists. We planned to set a date to begin interviewing prospects as soon as we returned from our next appointment...our first return visit to Penoaken. It had been five months since we left there; thus, almost two years would have passed and it would now be the year 2010. Our plan for returning to Penoaken was to take Illinois and America with us and to load up two additional Shetlands with our re-supply of primarily teaching and medical items.

Our arrival at Penoaken would be a surprise to Lori and Henry. They, of course, were not certain we would ever return and if we did they had no idea as to when it might be. We established the second week in November for our trip and that date was nearly upon us. We hurried our preparations, said goodbye to Heather, Jean, and Angus, and departed via the Easterly Bridge.

****

The weather was nice and when we crossed the bridge we had returned to the twenty-first century. Birds were singing and a breeze gently rustled the leaves. Everything appeared the same as we had left it.

For the first half of the journey, as the land was forested and rather uneven, we mostly walked and led our ponies. However, once we arrived at the meadow parking place, where we had left our vehicle before, we got aboard our trusty steeds and rode the final 9 miles. My cell phone no longer worked, so our arrival at the Travis Inn would be unheralded.

As we neared, things looked to be the same as when we left, and as we approached the rear entrance, I hollered, "Yo, Lori. Yo, Henry, ye ha' company. It be Freddy and Kenny. Coom ye forth."

Almost instantly the door opened and Lori rushed out, "Freddy, Kenny, oh my God. Is it really you?" I said, "Aye, Lori, and we be here to visit for a few days. Like me accent?" By now Henry appeared from the stables, saying, "Welcome home, lads, welcome ye back." We got off our ponies, hugged and kissed Lori, and hugged Henry saying, "Hey, guys, we are happy to see you two and to be here."

We went inside and headed directly to *The Pub* where Scotty was still holding forth and shouted, "Scotty, draw us the biggest ale in all o' the Highlands, with lotsa foam." Scotty responded, "Aye, lads, it be me pleasure, it be so good to see ye." Henry told Scotty to keep a tab and we would settle the bill later. We all adjourned to the large round table at the rear of the pub and chatted for awhile. Henry and Lori said they were full of questions and we told them we understood and would try to answer all of them.

I said, "The first order of business tomorrow will be for you to chauffer us around. We'll need to visit the bank and then purchase supplies which we will take back to aid us in the fields of learning and medicine. After that is done, we'll spend time talking about Auralee... You will find our story interesting." They responded they could hardly wait and added, "And we ha' a surprise for ye gentlemen as well."

They were smiling, almost giddy, like two children who had just robbed the cookie jar. I responded, "OK, you guys, we could use a good surprise, let us have it." Henry put his arm about Lori. We had never seen him do that before, and suddenly it hit us and we began to smile. Before we could get a word out, Henry said, "Gentlemen, we bring ye tidings o' good news. Since June 14th last, Lori be Mrs. Henry Travis. We were married in the kirk by thee good Reverend Seymour and the only thing missing be you lads and Auralee's records."

We were both elated, and asked Scotty to bring us another round. He replied, "Aye, be pleased to do so, lads; this one be on me." We all laughed. Ken and I gave Lori a kiss and shook Henry's hand vigorously. Both of us said our only disappointment was we did not come bearing gifts. Henry and Lori laughed and answered, "Thee be'en here, tha' be thee only gift we be needen." We thanked them, but added we would work on a gift.

Later we had dinner, a real twenty-first century feast, steaks, Jell-o and cottage cheese salad, parsley potatoes, lemonade, and a piece of cake which resembled tiramisu accompanied by a small scoop of rich vanilla ice cream. It was magnificent and we both were pleased. I remarked that it was best we not get used to such great food. After our meal we all said our goodnights; we were very tired. Henry said, "See ye at breakfast at, say seven?"

****

The next morning Ken and I left for Fort William with Henry in his pickup. It was the city nearby where we had opened our banking account. We visited the bank and withdrew five thousand dollars in equivalent British Pounds. If anything remained, Henry would redeposit it.

We visited the largest pharmacy in the city and spent two hours roaming the isles for over-the-counter drugs and items to fortify the small supply we originally took to Auralee. We purchased hot water bottles, some with syringes, thermometers, blood pressure apparatus, and all sorts of medicines. Our bill came to $1,450 dollars.

Next we went to a large store similar to Walmart where we stocked up on paper products, pencils, many types of teaching aides, solar equipment, and a few books for our small library. Total bill here $2, 200 dollars...grand total so far, $3,650 dollars.

After we finished I said to Henry, "We are treating for a giant ice cream sundae with nuts and whipped cream, maybe even two." Ken interjected, "Rather than two sundaes, let's make it a Pizza and a sundae." To which I quickly replied, "Excellent idea ole chap, let's do it." Henry just shook his head saying, "Think I willa just watch this performance." Following our feast we were stuffed but we reckoned, why not?

Driving back to Penoaken, Henry broached the broadening difficulties in the middle-east. Since we left, over two years ago, the "war" had worsened and was no longer limited to Afghanistan, Iraq, and with the Hezbollah in Lebanon.

It had spread to include rocket attacks, the bombing of Israel by Iran, plus major incursions by the Taliban into Afghanistan. Syrian backed attacks into the Golan Heights by the Hezbollah were increasing in depth and velocity.

Upon returning to the Inn, I asked Lori for old copies of their newspapers and luckily there was a supply which they had not thrown away. The editorials were specific and they sounded horrible.

Britain along with Australia, New Zealand, Italy, Poland, Canada, and a few of the Balkan counties were providing significant support in the efforts to stem the spread of Muslim fundamentalism. Pakistan, India, and Turkey were finding it increasingly more difficult to maintain their professed neutrality. Several Muslim countries, Egypt, Jordon, Kuwait, Bahrain, United Arab Emirates, Saudi Arabia were supportive but very evasive with that support. Russia and China remained giant power brokers desiring to be major players along with Iran and Syria in the Middle East.

Ken and I discussed what we learned from the papers and by talking with Lori and Henry. The two of us agreed the situation had grown critical. It seemed that by the time we returned to Penoaken on our next visit things could be horrible. So bad, we envisioned taking Lori and Henry back with us at that time to Auralee, if we could gain permission to do so. We could not now bring up this possibility with them. Upon our return to Auralee we would approach Angus and Reverend Dundee.

Over the next couple of days we relaxed, visited with Lori, Henry, Scotty, drove around the area in Henry's pickup, ate, and finally purchased two more Shetlands to carry our supplies back to Auralee.

Suddenly it was almost time to leave. We spent much of our last day telling them as much as we could about Auralee and how much we loved it. The next morning we said our goodbyes, promised we would be back in a couple of years, and hoped things in the world might be better. It was an appropriate thing to say, but Ken and I feared for the worst. Time would tell.

****

After loading our two new acquaintances named Travis and Penny, we packed our personal stuff aboard America and Illinois. Our ponies were loaded aboard Henry's 2 ½ ton truck for the trip to the meadow where we always parked, prior to entering the forested and hilly part of our journey. Before leaving we both gave Lori a kiss and once more told her and Henry how pleased we were about their wedding.

The journey with our four Shetlands was slow and it was late afternoon when we reached the place where the East Bridge should be, but it wasn't there? I turned to Ken and said, "Oh, oh, we got a problem, the bridge isn't here". He responded, "Oops." I suggested we have a sandwich and relax. I was certain Angus wouldn't let us down and after about an hour the bridge sure enough materialized. We were pleased to see Angus, Jean, and Heather waiting.

We had been away for about nineteen Auralee hours or nearly four days by twenty-first century time. We pulled and pushed our little caravan across the bridge, gave the girls hugs and kisses, and introduced them to our new friends, Travis and Penny. Our kennel was growing.

CHAPTER 16

TIME ALSO PASSES

SOON AFTER our return from Penoaken it was time to prepare for the Christmas Festival, which along with the Festival of Life each May, were Glen Auralee's two major festivals.

We also began working with Jean and Heather who had earlier submitted their lists of candidates who they believed would meet our requirements All candidates could read, cipher, and write with some varying degrees of aptitude. (10 teachers: 7 women and 3 men, and 6 medical assistants: 3 women and 3 men.) Angus, Jean, Heather, Ken and myself would constitute the selection committee and be the overall administrators of both programs. During the next two weeks we interviewed and passed favorably on all submitted candidates.

We immediately established an orientation program for the new candidates that outlined classroom and medical facility structures, and the positions they would fill within each of them. Soon Ken and I began training our assistants who all seemed excited, eager and willing to work diligently. We were pleased at the prospect for getting our two programs underway. Our new staffs would be assembled, evaluated, trained, and assigned to their most appropriate positions.

Classes for the first students would begin on January 5th, 1758, and we expected the first year to accept 56 students for all grades. Classes would be small to allow teachers to become comfortable in their new rolls as educators, counselors, and role models. Ken and I were both very pleased with the progress.

During this time we arranged for the construction of some things we needed: two wagons protected from the weather for the driver and occupants, two river boats designed for recreational cruising of Glen Auralee's rivers and coastline of the Norr Sea, and a small 7-9 hole golf course, restaurant, and meeting room. Angus was excited over the prospects of a golf course and said all these things could and would be done. He would set about finding men who could head them up.

Ken and I felt we had accomplished a lot since our return from Penoaken. We told Angus, Reverend Dundee, Jean, and Heather about our visit with Lori and Henry Travis, and the way people lived and worked in the twenty-first century. They of course were enthralled; however, we didn't include our concerns about how critical the world had become that we left only a couple years ago.

Privately we talked about approaching Reverend Dundee with the prospect of bringing Lori and Henry with us when we return from our next visit, should we find conditions significantly be worse.

****

Christmas and the festival was almost upon us and we all anxiously looked forward to it. December 24th arrived and the North Star appeared to us like the Star of Bethlehem must have looked to the three wise men. The square was adorned with decorations of all types and sizes. Each tent was trimmed with evergreen branches adorned with paper garlands of red, green, blue, yellow and white. The tallest pine tree in the square was also festooned with garlands, papier-mâché figures, and colored balls from top to bottom. The tents had seats for the people and were packed with food of all kinds. Entertainment was provided by story and fortunetellers accompanied by the pipers and fifers.

There were games to play of all kinds: races, lawn bowling, croquet, spin-the-wheel, and even one tent for cards and heather ale. Fortunately weather co-operated; clear, still, and the temperature 56 F degrees. The band piping traditional old Christmas songs, was accompanied by our kirk choir, and anyone who wanted joined in the singing. It was a joyous day and we were sorry to see it end.

****

Before we could sneeze, January 5th was here, the first day of school. Ken and Heather along with their ten teachers were ready. 56 students had registered: 24 in grades 1-3, 18 in grades 4-6, 8 in grades 7-9, and 6 in the 15+ class. 3 teachers were assigned to both the two larger classes, 2 to the 7-9 class, 2 to the 15+. A very large ratio of teachers to students was what Ken wanted to begin with. He had done his job well.

Meanwhile I had established my clinic in a couple of rooms and a storage shed at the kirk. The rooms were for now of adequate size and I would use one as a triage, the other as a patient room for any type of case from a backache to minor surgery. A recovery room space was sectioned off from this room.

I looked forward to the day, around March 15th, when the regular clinic might be ready. And when it arrived we hoped we were ready for anything, and brother did I get it…. Waiting at our front door was a neighboring crofter with a sick cow. I didn't turn him away, just quickly left him to be attended by one of my assistants who had knowledge of such things. It must have worked, the cow got better, and now the crofter wanted to adopt me as his son. Since we were available for house calls, time permitting, one medical assistant was assigned to Dee and another to Nevis. I have to admit my assistants picked up on what I had been preaching far beyond what was expected. These young folks were some really smart lads and lassies. Glen Auralee was going to benefit from what Ken and I had put in place.

****

Finally Ken and I had time to catch our breath and our thoughts again turned to Penoaken. We had previously agreed we would return every 5-6 months (25-30 months by time there). Since our first visit was made in November, 1757, our next visit would be due within the March to May 1758 time frame (April-September, 2012 in Penoaken). We reasoned it was now time to convene a meeting with Reverend Dundee, Angus, and their governing committee to present our request for bringing Lori and Henry Travis back with us from our next trip.

Angus talked with Reverend Dundee and set a time for the following week at the kirk. During that week Heather and Jean invited Ken and me on a picnic in the mountains north of Auralee. We were delighted and when we arrived Jean took us on a nature walk saying it was in preparation for a program she intended to introduce for the students. During the walk we became aware of just how in tune Jean was with the animals, birds, and flora. To say the least, Ken was ecstatic. Later we lunched on fried chicken, buttered bread, fruits, and washed it all down with some whole milk.

After lunch Jean dropped a bomb, "Freddy, my love, I ha' something to tell ye…. I be with child and expecten sometime in September and hope ye be happy as I be."…. I sat silently surprised and in shock for a moment, then stood, took her in my arms and stuttered, "Jean, dear bonnie Jean, I am happy all right, I am just out of my mind happy." Right away Ken turned to Heather, smiled, saying, "That's wonderful. I hope it happens to us someday." Heather laughed and said, "Aye, Kenny, my love, that be good…it already be happenen and we can expect an arrival at aboot the same time." Ken's eyes widened and his mouth dropped as he jumped to his feet, gave Heather a kiss and said, "Well why not, Fred, we always do everything at the same time don't we?"

The girls were radiant and giggled a lot, the rest of the day being spent on baby talk, like boy/girl, names, and so forth. On our way home we discussed how to tell Angus, who would boast and brag, and Jean's sister, Mary. As Heather had no parents, Angus had became her adopted father and as for Mary, we knew she would be delighted, but at the same time a little disappointed as she had not yet to be with child.

****

Now it was time for us to devote our efforts to our upcoming meeting with Reverend Dundee and his committee regarding the Henry and Lori question. I would make the presentation and as needed we both would respond to any questions. The committee consisted of Reverend Dundee, Angus, Mayors Bright, MacDougal, Frazier, and John Gregory, Angus's son-in-law. Reverend Dundee welcomed us, then asked me to present my request.

I arose, strode to the podium, and began, "Dear friends and fellow citizens of Glen Auralee, Ken and I are here today to ask your approval to invite two very worthy members of the twenty-first century to join in our fellowship here. Given it is possible at midnight on each May 14th for an outsider to cross into Glen Auralee, we only ask that when we next return from Penoaken we be permitted to bring two deserving folk here should they want to come. Who are these folks who Ken and I deem worthy of sponsorship?

"They are Lori and Henry Travis, owners of the Travis Inn at Penoaken. They are trustworthy, honorable, gracious and

Christian folk who have assisted Ken and me in our ability to restock our medical and teaching supplies which are benefiting the citizens here so greatly. It is Ken and my opinion that the world we once knew and lived in is fast approaching Armageddon and we do not wish to leave these deserving people to an undesirable fate. Lastly, should they elect to stay here with us, they would ask nothing from us except to be able to contribute to their new home with enthusiasm and vigor as Ken and I have. Thank you all for your attention."

Reverend Dundee thanked us and asked that we go to the fountain and wait until the committee had time to consider what we asked. We walked the short distance to the fountain, sat down, and I said, "Well, OK, ole friend, now we can only hope." Ken replied, "Yup, Fred, but no matter what, you did good." I smiled and nodded.

It took about 45 long, long minutes before John approached and said, "Ye now be wanted at the kirk." We couldn't tell anything by his demeanor so we just silently walked back and as we entered everyone appeared very solemn. I looked at Ken and said, "Oops, have I misjudged this thing?" Ken just squinted and said, "Don't know."

Reverend Dundee said, "Freddy, Kenny, lads, be ye here wi' me." Fear and trepidation was written all over our faces but we struggled forward to hear the verdict. He continued, "Lads, we ha' but two questions for ye." His remarks bolted through us like a rocket. That's all, two questions? Suddenly I was relieved and ready. Reverend Dundee smiled; I thought, *That was a good omen.* He said, "Ha' the folk asked to coom here by their own initiative? And if they nay ha' asked, then what will ye be tellen them?"

The questions seemed fair enough to me and I pondered my response before I began. "Reverend Dundee, the answer to your first question is no they have not asked us to come here. They have worked diligently in helping us maintain our source of supplies without prying, as you might expect good friends to do. We have never told them much about Auralee. At times I am certain their curiosity was overwhelming but they would not ask, assuming if the right time came we might confide in them.

"And now to your second question. Ken and I have concluded the time has arrived to broach this difficult question to them for their consideration. First being the condition of their world as it is rapidly changing. Ken and I are of the opinion their world is on the fast track to self destruction and it will cease to exist in a state which could maintain human life

"Should they accept our theory, we would explain the urgency of a decision. Though we return to Penoaken every 5-6 months by our time, actually 2 to 2 1/2 years would pass in Penoaken. We would tell them they must come with us now, on this trip, and we must be back to Auralee within four days.

"We would tell them more of Auralee and remind them it is Scotland in the year 1758 and is a small land with a limited population. That it is a land ordained and protected by God, has no crime, is not deceitful, and in total harmony with itself and nature. We would tell them that in our opinion they would love our simple life and find many interesting and important things to offer their new home. Finally after reaching Auralee, they would be granted 24 hours within which to make a decision to either remain or return to Penoaken. If they stay, Auralee would be their home forever, not affected by that which might happen in their old world. Finally, I would tell them it may sound impossible, but Auralee is for real, forever…. That, Sir, is what I would tell them."

Reverend Dundee thanked us and once more asked that we return to the square and wait for his beckon. Ken and I left and were pleasantly surprised to find Heather, Jean, and Mary waiting for us. They waved but remained quiet, awaiting us to say something.

Ken spoke, "Well, girls, it's over. Nothing more we can do now but wait." I was drained and apologized saying I just wanted to think. Everyone understood; the girls and Ken got up and walked around nearby. I truly appreciated the chance to recover my senses. It had been a tough go. I just sat listening to the water in the fountain. It was very soothing, almost mesmerizing. It reminded me of the water coursing over the rocks on the first night we found Auralee.

This time, John returned in only about twenty minutes and said, "Come on back, it's over." We gave the gals a kiss on their cheeks and walked silently back to the kirk. As we entered we were greeted with only smiles. I almost collapsed with pent up emotion. I concluded their response was positive and suddenly we were confronted again by Reverend Dundee who spoke, "Freddy, Kenny, it all be in ye favor. On ye next visit ye can wi' God's blessing ask Lori and Henry Travis to come to Glen Auralee." We thanked Reverend Dundee and all members of his committee. After leaving the church we met the girls at the square, told them of our great news, and they were delighted. Later I said to Ken, "OK, let's begin planning for our next trip to Penoaken, it'll be a dandy. We'll leave Auralee early on May 14, 1758 (2012 in Penoaken) and be back at the bridge before 11:59 PM on that same date." Ken agreed.

****

We had given our trip much thought. We would take America and Illinois with us, and should Henry and Lori came back, they would each bring their own Shetlands, plus two more for baggage. We would also obtain an additional pony for our last "horde" of medicines, etcetera, giving us a caravan of 7 horses. It would be a challenge, but we really had no other choice.

At all stages, time would be critical, there would not be time to hold back on decisions. It would be to come with us or not.... There would be no looking back, except for the 24 hour "bailout" period at Auralee. Ken added he was ready. I said, "Good, Ken, it is a done deal." We advised Angus and the girls and they seemed to understand. Over the next few days we spent our time constructing our trip, caring for our operations at the school and clinic, and spending time with our expectant mothers.

****

It was during the afternoon of May 1st, a rather cloudy and dreary day, when I noticed something very strange, very subtle, yet a noticeable sensory experience. The weather was heavy with only a light breeze, but it was taking on a rather unusual hue, a mixed pinkish and yellow overcast. I watched it intently for awhile and finally went to see Ken and asked if he had noticed anything strange about the weather.

He indicated he had not, as he had been indoors most of the day. When we went outside he studied the weather, looking from horizon to horizon, saying he too sensed something was unusual. "The color of the sky, I have never seen a sky like this before." As we talked, the skies continued to darken and now spasmodic flashes of light crisscrossed the sky from horizon to horizon. It was similar to lightening yet somehow seemed not the same. It was an extremely befuddling sight. As we watched the sky turned even a darker pink surrounded in an ominous sickly, yellowish background. The wind had increased and a light mist was falling. A sound like dull rolling kettle drums was added to the mix and people were becoming alarmed and frightened. I turned to Ken and said, "We are watching something unusual, but what does it mean?" I sensed it was a harbinger of something. But what? We did not know.

Shortly Angus and Reverend Dundee arrived in hopes we had some idea of what this phenomenon was. We replied, other than some sort of high altitude electrical disturbance (which meant little to them), we did not yet have the foggiest idea.

As the afternoon slowly crept by the storm, or whatever it was, for awhile worsened, but at around four o'clock it abated. It completely left and the sun regained it's presence.

Even the sounds of birds chirping returned. I told Angus and Reverend Dundee the show was apparently over and the storm was gone. I said, "It was a scary but heavenly demonstration put on by the all powerful presence, God. Perhaps it heralded that something ominous was happening outside of our world and had nothing to do with us." Evidently it worked and they left to spread the word.

I looked at Ken and said, "I have an idea of what it was we just saw.... It was the beginning of the end of time in the world outside of Glen Auralee and it came as an announcement to all who would destroy their environment, their world, and themselves. What do you think?" Ken studied my response for a few seconds and answered, "Damn it, Fred, I admire how analytical you can be sometimes. Of course that must be the answer. Lori and Henry will have experienced the same thing in Penoaken. It will have been the same in Chicago and all over the world for that matter. What will we tell the girls?" I responded, "Same thing we told Angus. Do you agree?" He gulped, "Yup."

CHAPTER 17

PENOAKEN LOST

WE SPENT the next few days recovering from the atmospheric experience. Nothing further had evidenced itself; thus, we readied our steeds and left Auralee for Penoaken at 6:00 AM on May, 14th . This would provide us 90 hours to complete work in Penoaken and still be back to the bridge at Auralee by midnight on May 14th.

Our route was familiar and thus we made good time, arriving at the meadow north of Penoaken at ten o'clock their time. The remaining distance should take us no more than 2½ hours making arrival at the Inn by early afternoon. We had no way to give any advance warning; thus, we had to rely on blind luck they would be at the Inn, or nearby.

We approached the Inn quietly, unnoticed. Ken and I dismounted, entered via the back door, arrived in the lobby, and encountered Scotty, the bartender. He told us he was the sole remaining employee of Henry and Lori. *The Pub* had long since closed and he was relegated to odd jobs working for room and board. He was so happy to see us and when asked how things were he shrugged his shoulders and replied, "Aye, Sirs, I be breathen. "I canna think o' anything good to be tellen ye." At this time Henry and Lori arrived and they screamed, "Freddy, Kenny, ye be here. Come sit wi' us, 'tis only terrible, terrible," and Lori began crying. Henry put his arm about her and said, "Now, now, dear, we donna want the boys to see us this way."

I said, "Henry, we want to know about your circumstances? We may have a solution for you. But first, do you have any newspapers or radio reports which would inform us about what is going on around the world?" Henry replied, "Freddy, the newspapers stopped a month ago, we nay longer ha' television, and we receive only periodic information over the radio. We do have a few old newspapers from a month or so ago ye can read." I continued, "Yes, may we have them to study?" He replied, "Of course."

Ken and I sat around a large coffee table in the lounge. We read and reread the most horrific accounts of what was going on around the world. We could have never imagined them. My first reaction was *come on now, this can not be true.*

****

During 2011 The United States completed withdrawal from Iraq, Kuwait, Bahrain, and Afghanistan. Iran immediately invaded and took control of all oil fields and assigned territorial rights to their allies, the Taliban.

At this time Russia deployed troops to the Arctic, thus controlling the immense oil reserves. Even more dastardly she fired several atomic missiles upon Oahu, Hawaii, once again surprising and destroying the US Fleet anchored at Pearl Harbor. The entire island was mercilessly turned into a catastrophic mess. Thousands were killed or died from atomic fallout. Oil costs skyrocketed to well over $600 dollars a barrel; thus, even when available it was priced beyond the reach of the vast majority in Europe and North America. Even fuel to the military was stringently rationed.

Over 12,000,000 illegal immigrants from Mexico, Central, and South America were granted citizenship in the United States with some 40% immediately qualifying for welfare assistance as recipients of a massive Universal Health Plan. Taxes were increased to 60% for all incomes over $250,000 annually.

The president sent his Secretary of State to Iran for discussions with Ahmadinejad, and returned with a bundle of promises including *Peace in Our Time,* an old Chamberlain quote from 1938.

The much weakened U.S. Navy was rushed recklessly to the aid of Israel, and was mostly destroyed by the combined air forces of Russia, Iran, and Syria. Our once superior aircraft carriers were left at home lacking the necessary fuel and support vessels to venture that far away from home waters.

India went to war with Pakistan and atomic warheads plummeted to earth in both directions filling the atmosphere with poisonous radiation fallout which was carried worldwide by the air currents. No place was immune. The story went on infinitum. I was sick at my stomach. My thoughts immediately turned to Mom, Dad, Sue Ellen, Samantha, and the gang back at work. I wondered if they were still OK.

Quickly I readjusted to the task at hand and asked Lori if she had anything to eat and drink. She responded, "Aye, a bit and a little ale, I think." We sat and each of us slowly consumed a slice of warmed over sausage snuggled between two thin slices of very course bread, half an apple, and a pint of ale served up by Scotty. A far cry from the sumptuous offerings once served at the Travis Inn.

I asked Henry what his plans were and he softly said, "We dinna ha' any plans, lads, only to wait here to die and pray a miracle might happen. There nay be any place to go and we nay believe any miracle be comen." How sad it made us feel, but that was a perfect opening. I said, "Lori, Henry, perhaps your prayers can be answered.

"In the past we have told you some things about Auralee, but there is much more you should know. Henry, Lori, listen to me closely...*for it may be possible for you to return there with us from this world of chaos.*" Their eyes brightened. Both were excited at the possibility of leaving, and asked, "Will ye be tellen us more?"

I began, "Henry, Lori, Auralee exists in the Highlands of Scotland in the year 1758. It is the place reported by Haggis Frisbee to the church in the year 1755 of a village which disappeared from the earth. Now I will tell you what we told the folks in Auralee that we would say to you.

"It is a land of about 34 square miles in size with a population of about 1,000 people. It is a land ordained and protected by God, has no crime, is not deceitful, and in total harmony with itself and nature. In our opinion you would both love the simpler life there and find many interesting and important things to do. Finally, after reaching Auralee you would have 24 hours to make your decision to either remain or return to Penoaken.

"If you stay, Auralee will be your home forever away from a world, your world and our old world, which is no longer a place that can be resurrected. Auralee is a place beyond anything that is your old world. The only issue now is your decision to go with us and time is constrained. We must be back to Auralee soon."

Henry turned to Lori and said, "Honey, as scary as it may be, I believe we must accept Freddy and Kenny's offer. We be both convinced this world be beyond any help other than divine intervention." Lori looked at us and sobbed, "Aye, Freddy and Kenny, I be o' the same feelen as Henry. We dinna have any choice, but we canna leave here wi'out Scotty. He be our dearest and most loyal friend and we canna leave him here. He would die without us."

I looked at Ken, softly said, "We have a dilemma here, Ken. Lori, give us a few moments and we'll be back as soon as we have an answer for you." She replied, "Oh, thank ye, we be waiten." We left for the bar and managed to pour ourselves a small ale; it was evident the keg was all but empty. Ken said, "What are we to do? We have no authority to take another person back with us." I said, "Ken, you are right, but consider we will be arriving at midnight May 14, 1758. What does that suggest?"

Immediately he saw where I was going and replied, "*The portal is open, the portal is open.*" I answered, "Yeh, and the only retort Angus could have would be Scotty did not find the bridge on his own, we helped him. Now I do not propose he will raise that objective, but should he, we will just have to throw ourselves on the *mercy of the court* so to speak. Worth a try, ole boy?" Ken smiled, took a small swig on his ale, and said, "Let's have a go at it."

We returned to a very somber Henry and Lori. Ken excitedly told them we would ask Scotty to go with us. We could not guarantee his deliverance, but believed his chances were good, otherwise we would just say no.

"Henry, you and Lori talk to him and make certain he wants to come along and that he understand the finality of his decision if he does." Henry jumped up and exclaimed, "We thank ye, lads, from the bottom o' our hearts. We shall talk wi' Scotty." They left immediately and within fifteen minutes were back with smiles all over and Scotty in tow. "Aye, Scotty wants to go, we thank ye, and Scotty thanks ye. We love ye."

****

I said, "It's settled; tomorrow morning Ken and I will outline what we need to have completed by the time we depart for Auralee. With all the baggage we will have and a caravan of 9 or

10 Shetlands it will be an effort." Henry answered, "It willa work, we willa make it work."

I replied, "You bet it will, Henry. Now let's turn in and get an early start in the morning, say at five o'clock. I have only one question, Henry, will you have any problem obtaining 7 or 8 ponies?" He thought for a minute and said, "No, I dinna think so, we still ha' four here at the Inn." We said goodnight and figured sleep would be difficult. I hoped everyone had an ample supply of adrenalin.

Our first day was taken up by readying the ponies and harness for the trip, securing two trucks which would transport us and the ponies to the meadow nine miles north of the Inn, and laying out our plans for securing our supplies.

From the morning after we arrived, for the next 2 days (Penoaken time), Ken and Henry traveled in one vehicle, Lori and myself in a second. Scotty stayed behind in charge of packing the containers as we returned with supplies. He also had to scrounge up enough food to sustain us until we got to Auralee. We knew if anyone could do it Scotty would be the one.

We were somewhat surprised that our bank was still honoring limited withdrawals and after withdrawing what we could, we traveled to every village and city, regardless of size, within a radius of twenty miles. Everything was scarce and costly. At five o'clock on our departure morning we took one final look around. Bless her heart, Lori, had our breakfast ready, our last meal at the *Travis Inn at Penoaken*.

I was embarrassed by the meagerness of our last breakfast and of the food we would have for our journey. Obviously we hadn't arrived here too soon, but we made no comment.

Over the last few days Lori had used everything she had available. For breakfast we each had one fried egg, two pieces of coarse bread, one with some butter and a little jam, a half sausage patty, half an apple, and a small glass of milk. Our meals for the trip consisted of one apple apiece, one sandwich with a thin slice of cheese, a small slice of bacon, one hard boiled egg, and a thermos of milk.

Lori sobbed, "I be sorry Freddy and Kenny, it be all we ha' left in our larder. We just be liven day-by-day." We answered, "Lori, dear Lori, the meals are magnificent and you owe us no apology. It will suffice nicely until we reach Auralee."

****

It was now 6:00 AM and time to leave Penoaken behind us forever. It was impossible for Ken and I to imagine Henry, Scotty, and Lori's sadness of leaving, yet excited by their prospects of finding a new world full of hope. Their emotions would fill an ocean…. They stood transfixed looking about at the lake, the ducks, the little marble markers of the two young lovers from William Wallace's era, and the Inn. Finally, Henry said, "It be time to go. We nay tarry on our mission." Scotty replied, "Aye." Lori only sobbed.

The horses were packed and loaded aboard the trucks for our journey to the clearing; from there the difficult part of our trip would start, foraging through the forest and over the hills for seven plus miles to Auralee. Five of our ponies were lightly loaded in order for us to ride them when the land permitted, and five were loaded to the hilt with everything we could cram aboard them.

Included in our inventories were two small Geiger counters, all the medical and teaching supplies we could find room for, a 1900 and 2006 world atlas, a book of Scotland's birds, trees, and flowers, medical charts, binoculars, mechanical clocks, two bathroom scales, small tools, some seasoning herbs to plant, and some trinkets for Jean, Heather, and Mary. Henry, Lori and Scotty had items such as boots and clothing to contend with. It had been a formidable task, but we did it. At the last minute I took the broadsword of Robert de Bruce from the wall and slung it on America's back. Damn thing was heavy, but I wanted it as a gift for Angus.

Our trip went smoothly covering the 16 plus miles to our tree stump in a little over 11 hours. It was almost five o'clock as we approached the location where the East bridge should be. It would be dark soon and I knew we would have to wait until midnight.

We tethered and fed the ponies, found our stump, and settled down for our last meal in the twenty-first century. All we had left were 3 apples, six pieces of bread, about a pound of cheese, and a little milk. Spartan, but it would do until, we hoped, Angus and Auralee would come to our rescue. Everyone was exhausted; thus, we laid back on our bed rolls and tried to doze off. One person was left awake at all times. Didn't want to sleep past midnight.

At 11 o'clock we were up checking on the ponies and assuring that all was ready. The last hour dragged by and no one had much to say. Suddenly, it was 11:55 PM on the evening of May 14th (Auralee time) and it was still ominously quiet. The only sound we heard was our heavy breathing.

Then very quietly at first, then louder, came the sound of water running over a rapid, birds singing in the distance, and the path leading up to the bridge appeared. I hollered, "Okay, folks, we are home. Get the ponies and follow me." Shortly we could see several forms standing across the bridge at the entrance to Auralee…. It was Angus along with Jean, Heather, Mary, and John Gregory. We waved and shouted, "We are home and have company with us."

They returned our greeting and replied, "Welcome home, Freddy and Kenny, we bid ye new citizens o' Auralee greetings; coom ye forth." Our caravan trudged slowly and quietly across the bridge. Ken and I threw our arms about Angus and the girls saying, "We are glad to be home." Henry and Lori were crying with happiness. Scotty was quiet, hoping he would not be noticed.

CHAPTER 18

ETERNITY BEGINS

A FTER WE introduced everyone to Henry, Lori, and Scotty, Ken and I immediately called Angus aside. I said, "Angus, obviously you see we have an extra person with us, Scotty. We appreciate you having not brought up that fact. He has for years been a devoted member of Henry and Lori's family. It would have been cruel and inhuman to just pack up and leave him. I truly doubt he would have survived for long. We greatly hope this will not be a problem for you, since he did arrive here during the time Auralee's portal was open."

Angus replied, "Aye, Freddy, I noticed your addition. I canna give ye a final answer, but I will present ye case to Reverend Dundee." Ken and I thanked Angus, and returned to our group.

We proceeded to Auralee. On the way we talked to our new citizens about everything as we passed: the mountains, the pastures with their sheep and cattle being herded by the ever present and friendly sheep dogs, the temperate climate, the friendly folk, and about our Elder, Reverend Dundee. Our trip took a little over an hour. When we arrived at Angus's home several citizens helped us remove our supplies, store them in the barn, and return America and Illinois along with the new ponies to Freddy's corral. Angus also had three carts hitched and ready for our use. Before we began our introduction excursion, Angus asked if we be hungry and Ken answered for us all. "Yes, Sir, we be very hungry." As always Angus had anticipated our need and had tables set up. As soon as we washed, several ladies of the Glen started delivering our snack…an Auralee snack: fried chicken, ham, cheeses, mashed potatoes with cream gravy, warm buttered sweet bread, several choices of vegetables, heather ale, milk, and finally warm apple pie.

Ken and I watched as Henry and Lori's eyes popped wide open. They were amazed, very hungry, and dove right in. After we finished, Henry spoke first, "We be extremely surprised. This be the finest and best prepared home cooken we ha' ever had. We thank ye one and all." Scotty and Lori raised their cups in a toast gesture, and Angus replied, "Ye be welcome. Now we must begin our tour of Glen Auralee as time be passen."

We boarded our "Auralee limousines." Angus, Henry, Ken, and Mary in the lead, followed by me, Lori, and Jean, with John, Scotty, and Heather bringing up the rear cart. Our path took us first through the square where, being it was May 15th ,the Festival of Life was in full swing. The band was piping such tunes as *Bonnie Auralee* and *Tak Ye High Rood*. Folks were dancing, singing, drinking heather ale, playing games, and generally having a good-old-time. We explained the Festival of Life occurred every May 15th and that there were several other gala festivals held in the square throughout the year,

We passed the golf course and club house (still under construction), went by my clinic and Ken's school, stopped at the bakery for a cookie, and then headed for the countryside. Glen Auralee life never looked better. Streets and lawns were clean and neat, flowers were in bloom everywhere, and the birds were in their finest voice.

While in the countryside we passed Ken and Heather's croft and Cindy ran to greet us. Next we visited Nevis and were greeted by Mayor MacDougal who welcomed the new citizens to his towne and presented them with some cookies from the towne bakery. Lori commented she would be putting on weight at this rate. There weren't many people around; I pointed out they were all at the festival. From Nevis we swung east past the dairy farm. Here too it was rather quiet.

Only a few hands were working and sheep dogs were very active. We pointed out this was where the Glen's supply of good milk and cheeses came from. From here we returned to Auralee, passing more fields of crops, sheep, and cattle.

At Auralee we stopped at the festival for a pint of heather and a sausage sandwich before climbing back aboard our "limos." We next visited Reverend Dundee's home where he greeted us with a smile and a friendly wave.

He shook everyone's hand and said, "Ye be very welcome to stay wi' us." I was very relieved that his welcome apparently included Scotty. (Angus had managed to get the word to him that there would be an extra guest.) "We be very proud o' our Glen. It be a small world, but we be a very happy and merry folk. Should ye ha' any questions Angus, Freddy, or Kenny canna answer, ye coom see me."

He smiled graciously and we re-boarded our carts. From here we crossed the North River bridge near the little resort in the mountains where Jean and I had our honeymoon. This had to be the most beautiful view in the whole Glen. Pristine mountains, blue sky, birds singing, and in the distance the valley spread out before us. I said, "Gotta admit, it's pretty spectacular." Henry, Lori and Scotty all agreed they were very impressed with all they had seen.

Following a short rest, we mounted our carts and returned to Auralee. On the way we visited a small neighborhood of farming crofts whose primary functions were pasturing and raising herds of sheep and cattle. Their community consisted of three men, three women, and six children ranging in ages from 2 to 13 years in age. Since Auralee was only about a mile and a half away, their lives pretty much hinged around it, and two of the children, ages 6 & 8 were in classes at Ken's school. Everyone was excited to meet such important visitors from beyond their world and wished them welcome. We continued, passing once more through the square where activities were well underway.

****

We arrived at Angus's home at 2:30. Although Henry, Lori, and Scotty had until midnight to depart Auralee should they choose to do so, it would be important they cross the bridge by 4:30 as it would be dark within the hour and they would need to establish a camp in the forest for the night.

****

We got off our ponies, took a seat at a long table. Angus was first to speak. "It be me hope that ye ha' a good impression o' our wee and bonnie world. Ye be very welcome to stay, and we hope ye will. I be sorry ye ha' not more tyme to make ye decision." I added, "Ken and I want to add our feelings to what Angus just told you.

"We have been through the change of coming to a land some 250 years past. It was not simple to do, but we hasten to tell you we are not sorry. Sure we miss many things about the twenty-first century, but that world is dying and you no longer belong there. We hope the three of you will let it go and stay here with us."

After a moment Henry spoke. "We canna thank ye all enough. The three o' us would like a few moments to confer and we be given ye our answers in a few minutes." They walked to a nearby park and sat under a large tree. I commented to the remaining group, "Nice going everyone. You did a great job and I have no doubts but that our friends will stay here."

Henry, Lori, and Scotty returned in about twenty minutes, and Henry spoke. "Angus, Sir, Freddy, and Kenny, we be eternally thankful to ye for our deliverance. We look forward to becomen good and useful citizens of Auralee." We all hugged and shook hands and told them we were so very happy of their decisions.

****

Until permanent quarters could be provided, Angus agreed Lori and Henry could use Mary's well used room. Ken and Heather would "adopt" Scotty until he could find a more permanent place.

Angus continued, "We be happy for ye and for us. Ye no longer belong to thee old world and now be citizens o' Glen Auralee. The 15th o' May in the year o' our Lord, 1758 be thee first day o' ye new life. There still be tyme to return to and enjoy ye first Festival o' Life."

****

At the festival it was introductions, welcomes, toasts and singing. I was certain our new citizens would not remember the names of many of the folks they met. I took the opportunity to talk with Edward and Celia McNairy who ran the dairy farm, and discussed Scotty with them. They graciously offered to have him stay with them to learn the business of managing livestock and making cheese and dairy products which were important assets to Auralee's life. I later talked with Scotty who was pleased with the opportunity.

Over the next two days we escorted our three new citizens about the remainder of Glen Auralee, the village of Dee, the North

Island, and were cordially welcomed at several crofts. Everyone seemed to be getting used to their new surroundings, and time slid by quickly.

****

Suddenly it was July, both Heather and Jean looked very much as if they were approaching their expected motherhood, and on July 7th Jean delivered a bonnie wee lass we named Tiffany Marie (after Jean's mother), and Heather followed on the 18th with Benjamin James, or BJ (after her father).

There was excitement everywhere over the new citizens who held dual citizenship to the eighteenth and twenty-first centuries. Angus even designed an emblem for them to wear on their tartans…an American flag with the Scottish tilted white cross in a field of Scottish blue in place of the stars. Ken, Heather, Jean and I were pleased with the design, and told Angus, "Dad, you are beyond the greatest and your grandchildren will make you very proud of them." He didn't say anything but we could see through the tears in his eyes he was gratified. There was so much love, understanding, and knowledge crammed into this man.

With each passing day, Tiffany and BJ seemed to grow, and suddenly they had both taken their first steps to the delight of everyone. They were becoming celebrities. Tiffany had black hair, sparkling brown eyes, great smile, and was cute as she could be. On the other hand BJ was blonde, blue-eyed, and handsome. It was obvious we had an outstanding twosome aboard our ship-of-life and they would bear watching.

****

While all this was occurring, months rushed by and suddenly it was May 1761 in Auralee, and the year 2033 in Penoaken. It was time for Ken and me to assess the status of the twenty-first century. Would it still be feasible to obtain more goods to stockpile our dwindling supplies, or had the worst happened? We quickly packed our supplies on America and Illinois, including our most important pieces of equipment, our Geiger counters. Three years had passed since we last visited Penoaken; we did imagine significant changes had taken place.

On May 20th Angus, Ken and I arrived at the East Bridge and I said to Angus, "Well, here we go into who knows what. Wish us well." He retorted, "Aye, lads, but are ye sure o' wha' ye be doen?" I replied, "Aye, Angus, we do not know for certain what we may find when we pass beyond the bridge, but we must find out."

Having said our piece we slowly turned, looked at each other, and without words put on our leather coverings, which for a short interval of time would hopefully ward off ambient radiation. With our Geiger counters pointing ahead of us we gingerly crept across the East Bridge into the unknown. Amazingly the outside world was never seen from Auralee and inversely Auralee was not visible except for 24 hours each May 15th from the outside world.

All of a sudden we were across.... *It was like nothing...as though we opened the door and no one was there.* Desolation and a sudden absence of color slammed us in the face. Trees were but barren stumps, there was no grass, the sky was a solid dull gray, no sound, not even birds, or even a breeze. It looked as if we had entered a dead world, and our Geiger counters were chattering, indicating a level of radioactivity that would be harmful to us if we remained exposed for more than three hours. Obviously we could not continue to Penoaken. I said to Ken that we should continue on for about a half hour and then return to Auralee. He agreed.

We ventured on, continuing to see nothing but bareness. Apparently the world had destroyed itself and was lying inert beneath a blanket of radioactive fallout. It would require at least another fifteen years (three years Auralee time) for radiation levels to dissipate to levels which would be safe for further incursions toward Penoaken.

After about an hour and fifteen minutes I said, "Ken, let's get the hell out of here. We'll document what we have seen today and set our sights to return three years from this date, May 1764 (2043 Penoaken time)." Ken's comment was, "Amen, brother, let's get out of this place ASAP." When we crossed back over the bridge to Auralee, Angus was still there. It had been less than forty minutes since we departed.

Ken was in the lead and quickly removed his protective gear announcing, "Hey, Angus, we are back, that place is doomsday." I added, "Yep, Ken is right and we will explain it to you on the way home. I suggest we initially tell only Reverend Dundee, Henry, Lori, Scotty, Jean and Heather of what we found. Then shortly follow with a meeting to disseminate what we saw and how it happened. What we tell them will be difficult for eighteenth century folk to absorb."

Ken and I documented our brief visit as best we could, let our leather clothing hang in the wind several days until the radiation count had returned to zero, and tried to prepare ourselves for the upcoming meeting.

****

Reverend Dundee and Angus didn't wait long and the meeting was set four days hence. We would be ready and hoped we could make some sense to the folk out of something beyond their comprehension. I prayed we could and, as usual, the story telling fell upon me. I really didn't care. Ken was always in support and that was OK by me.

The time for our *day of infamy* report arrived. It was a glorious day which heralded a large turnout. The meeting was held at the Auralee kirk and it was jam packed.

Reverend Dundee was brief in his introduction saying only, "My good folk, Master Freddy ha' a difficult story to be tellen. It be a horrible tale he tells. Freddy, lad, I pray for ye as I be prayen for all the folk back in Penoaken." Slowly and with noticeable effort I walked to the front of the kirk. The room was unearthly silent and without so much as a thank you, I just started.

"It is with great humility and sorrow that I am here today. You must accept what I am about to tell you with open hearts and minds for you will not be prepared for what you hear. Imagine that in the 250 some years that had gone by until my time in the twenty-first century many advances in every aspect of life had advanced to levels which would amaze and confuse you. I will deal today with only one area…war and destruction.

"Machines we call airplanes could fly miles high in the sky and drop giant explosive bombs on the earth below them. At the same time scientists had produced the ability to shoot massive rockets for thousands of miles across oceans which also carried massive explosives to drop upon the towns and countryside below. These explosive devices were so powerful they could wipe out life of all kinds: people, animals, trees, and flowers over a distance of 20 to 35 miles in all directions. Yet, this be only a part of the effects of these bombs.

"The explosions created a deadly dust, very small particles much smaller than even a grain of fine sand. They were then thrown back into the upper air and carried by air currents for hundred of miles to drop back to earth as a deadly rain.

"Many countries throughout the world had these weapons of mass destruction and as they threatened each other, they began to unleash these terrible weapons. As time passed the atmosphere, that is the air, became a deadly poison to absolutely every living thing.

"That is what Ken and I found…. To the best of our knowledge as time passed, everyone on the earth died…except for we here in Glen Auralee. We are perhaps now the only living things in the world. It is now up to you to continue living as you have been doing since your deliverance.

"Ladies and gentlemen of Glen Auralee, Kenny and I pray you will accept what I have done my best to explain to you. May we all continue with our lives and be thankful that we are so chosen." I was shaken but able to walk to the front of the church and out the door followed closely by Ken, Angus, Lori and Henry Travis, Scotty, Jean, Heather, and John and Mary Gregory.

I left Reverend Dundee alone to close the proceedings, which I understand he did with great tact. Saying finally, "Aye, ye o' faith remember it be God's way. The end o' thee world as it first be put together be always prophesized. Remain ye humble and deserven."

It was extremely difficult to put the last crossing back to the twenty-first century out of our minds, but that was exactly what Ken and I had to do to the best of our abilities.

****

Meantime there were projects which had been ongoing for the past 16 months: the design and construction of two covered wagons to use as transportation for medical cases. This project was now complete. Next the design and construction of two pleasure boats to ply the rivers and coastline of Glen Auralee; this project was also complete. Finally the design and building of a small golf course, Angus's project it was called. It too, along with a clubhouse, was ready for dedication and it was decided, guess what, a festival should precede the opening; thus, one was set for June 1st to be followed by the first day of golf play on June 4th.

On June 4th, Angus, Reverend Dundee, Ken and I would be the first foursome. The course consisted of 5 holes with two additional holes planned for the future. Par would be 24 with holes of 4,5,6,4,5 which allowed for the slowness of the course and the rolling characteristics of the golf balls and clubs. However, we did invent a wooden tee which helped a little. All-in-all, not exactly professional level, but it would be fun.

The clubhouse had a lunch room, a main room with a dance floor and fireplace, a bar called *The Pub* in honor of the one at the Travis Inn at Penoaken, and a kitchen area with a large fireplace. In total the clubhouse could accommodate up to 75 guests. Outdoors the planted grounds included a park with tables for picnics, a playground, and a dock for the pleasure craft was located nearby, rather a nice effort by Angus and his talented team of workers.

On June 1st the Festival of Fun was held and the speeches were many, but short. They included Reverend Dundee, who delivered the dedication, Angus, William Wells, the foreman, John Gregory, Mayors Bright, Frazier, and MacDougal, Ken, and myself. Everyone enthusiastically cheered each speaker and the pipes played, of course, *Bonnie Auralee.*

The great day had arrived, June 4th. The golf course was crowded in anticipation of Auralee's first ever golf game. Over 200 people attended, inside and out; we were barely able to accommodate everybody.

In addition to the Mitchell, Effington, Reverend Dundee and Macgregor foursome, two additional foursomes made up from local dignitaries would provide the talent, or at least the laughs. We had all been practicing with Ken and I providing the *teaching*, if I can use the word loosely.

Although the game of golf had been widely played in Scotland for well over 300 years, it had never been seen in Glen Auralee. Perhaps that was one reason for their maintained piety! But now... the wood was about to meet the turf. June 4th, a nice day, a great audience, and 12 excited Highland gentlemen were "ready" for the historic first ever game. By necessity the rules were basic and simple; of course, we were all sworn to abide by them.

A word of amazement about the equipment must be entered here: Balls were leather spheres tightly stuffed with feathers. Golf clubs included a putter, a driving club, and a pitching club for shorter approaches to the "hole," where a white flag stuck out denoting it's location. Club design was a wooden shaft with leather grip, a wooden club head connected to the shaft and bound tightly with leather bindings. I laughingly thought, *Anyone for golf?*

The great event arrived, and as the pipes quieted it was time for the first tee off. Angus led the way followed in order by Reverend Dundee, Ken and me. His first swing wasn't too bad, sorta down the fairway about 35 yards. Reverend Dundee with heavenly demeanor swung mightily off to the right a wee bit. The first slice in history of Glen Auralee Golf Course. Ken was next and drove his ball right down the center, got a fair roll, for a lengthy 60 feet. I was next and hooked my ball considerably to the left about 50 feet. Everyone cheered. Scores for the par 4 first hole were 7,7, 6, and 8.

The scores piled up and the gallery followed us around the course with at least a semblance of dignity. When the final scores for the first 5 hole round in history were posted, they read: Effington (33), Mitchell (34), Macgregor (37), Dundee (41). Everyone laughed and cheered and the good reverend took it all in good faith. He commented, "With thee grace o' thee ole mighty, I will prevail. I be needen a wee bit more tyme."

The fun, games, and dancing continued into the evening. All in all it was a very festive day and we were certain golf had finally come

to Auralee. During the evening Ken made an announcement…
he had perfected a recipe for…*PIZZA*! He would display his
new creation at the mid-summer festival next month which he
named the Festival of Pizza. Everyone cheered in anticipation of
the forthcoming event.

Ken's recipe for his Pizza was: roll out a medium thin pie dough
on a large cast iron cooking sheet, add layers of cheese, between
the cheese add small chunks of sausage, bacon, chopped onions,
green peppers, sprinkle heartily with dill weed, rosemary, salt,
and black pepper. Place in baking oven at a hot heat and bake
for 15-20 minutes. Slice resulting pie into six servings and place
each on a warm wooden plate. Serve with adequate amounts of
heather ale.

The Festival of Pizza arrived and there was no way we could stay
up with the demand. It took off like a Roman candle. I wasn't
certain Ken had done the good citizens of Glen Auralee any favor
for I expected their average weight would increase significantly.
Anyway the craze of the twentieth century had officially arrived
in eighteenth century Auralee.

At the festival we also introduced the two cruise boats which were
to ply the coastline and inland waterways on special occasions.
Each would carry up to eight adult passengers, had a crew of
eight rowers, a helmsman, a steward, and a captain. Light snacks
would be available plus ale for adults. The trips would last 5-6
hours and include a picnic served along the way by local crofters.
Specials trips would be offered to the schools for nature trips.

****

Over the course of the following three years, Ken's school and my
medical clinic did quite well. Ken's graduating students began to
take their place in the ranks of Auralee's leading citizens.

Time to revisit Penoaken was again approaching. It was now April 1767 and we agreed to leave in May for our revisit at which time fifteen years would have passed in the twenty-first century. It would be 2057 and we estimated the radiation levels would be low enough by now for us to be safe.

Tiffany and BJ were now eight, very alert and active youngsters, but not yet old enough to understand what our leaving meant. Scotty had learned a new trade at the dairy farm and had married a local lass, Christine Fowler. She had given birth to a fine son, Harry, now 6 years old.

Lori and Henry managed the golf course, clubhouse, and cruise line. Scotty worked with them on special occasions. Things were moving right along. By now the local citizenry had forgotten our last trip to Penoaken; three years had passed.

CHAPTER 19

ARMAGEDDON

K<small>EN</small>, H<small>ENRY</small>, Scotty, Lori and I finalized our plan for returning to Penoaken. After Ken and my last attempt to visit Penoaken, we did not hold out hope that we would find anything comforting. But this was an effort we all had to make and were as ready as we would ever be.

It was a lovely day in Glen Auralee as our little caravan of seven ponies and five fearful people crossed the East Bridge into the twenty-first century. What greeted us was a repeat of what we had seen three years earlier (Auralee time). A dismal flat dispassionate gray nothing, no living thing. Trees were without leaves, no grass, and no weeds. There were no sounds, only nothingness pushed at us like a massive steel blob. It truly was frightening. The only thing here was emptiness, So far nothing had changed. In the fifteen years (Penoaken time) since our last visit not even a green sprout.

Ken and I immediately activated our Geiger counters. They would be our constant companions for the duration of our stay. Fortunately, our first good news, the radiation level read in the low range. We found a lot of erosion from rain, evidence that nature was still around.

We continued riding our ponies as we made our way through what once had been a densely wooded area full of vibrant life. Now the only evidence that life ever existed here were the barren remnants of trees and disintegrating wooden fences. We continued toward Penoaken; Henry, Lori, and Scotty were very somber, stunned at what we were seeing.

After five hours of passing only desolation, we arrived at the meadow that intersected with the trail to Penoaken, still nine miles distant. We paused for lunch. Our Geiger counters were still indicating low radiation.

After 40 minutes we mounted our steeds and continued passing barren meadows which at one time had been full of blooming heather. To some degree all of us were crying and after 3 hours, in the distance, we saw the *Travis Inn at Penoaken*, a crushing experience for Lori, Henry, and Scotty. It took everything Ken and I could do to calm them. We stopped our caravan for twenty minutes while they regained their composure. When we entered the grounds of the Inn, the sight they saw did nothing to help them keep the confidence they were just beginning to find.

At 3:00 PM Ken suggested we set up camp in the yard, wait until morning before going inside, and after that check out the village. Everyone agreed.

We tethered our ponies, pitched our tents, and started a fire using some really dry wood. The roof of the Inn appeared still intact, several windows were missing but most remained dirty but unbroken. The doors looked to be in place.

A light rain was falling, the temperature had dropped to a chilly 48 degrees Fahrenheit, and was getting colder. We would need to establish a fire watch tonight if we wanted to keep the "home" fires burning. Our tents and blankets would keep us reasonably warm, and the fire would at least make us feel warmer and more secure. Fortunately during the night the weather cleared. We could see stars, the first familiar and comforting thing we had seen.

****

After breakfast Henry, Lori and Scotty rushed to get inside the Inn; Ken and I followed close behind. Inside it was cold and dark. It was damp, yet there was no smell of mold. Evidently mold could not even survive. The only light entered from windows and doors that were open. It was exceedingly morose and depressing. We toured the interior of the Inn from top to bottom.

Things seemed rather well preserved, though rather worn and dried after all these years. The records still were where Henry and Lori had left them. Lori's old chair still sat behind her desk and she patted it lovingly. We entered the *Pub,* Scotty's old lair. The bar, displaying all it's resplendent bottles and glasses covered with a good layer of dust, otherwise looked ready for customers.

We next toured the grounds, past the gracious pond where ducks, geese, and swans once welcomed guests to the *Inn*. It was still full of water but had no occupants, no flowers, grass, or trees surrounded it. How sad everything was. The headstones marking the resting place of the two lovers were standing aloof among erosion and dirt. Yet, the inscriptions were still visible.

After leaving the *Inn*, we walked by homes and business places which were once part of a vibrant and thriving community. It was evident the village of Penoaken had been quickly abandoned as it was void of any remains of the population or their animals. The population evidently packed up and left in mass taking everything they could with them. But where did they go? We looked, but found no clues. We ventured inside several houses and business places.

Everything appeared in good order, as if on call, everyone took their portable belongings and just left. We found nothing which could aid us in search for answers, except all cars, trucks, and tractors were absent suggesting the population may have used them in traveling some distance.

We had great difficulty coping with the bleakness and sheer dismalness of the place. It left us with a very hollow, haunting feeling. Lori was sobbing again, and I could sense Henry and Scotty were also having sorrowful feelings.

I turned to Ken and said, "You know, ole friend, the whole world must be like this. Chicago, Samantha, the club, my family, our friends, gone, just like here." He replied, "Yup, Fred, I am afraid you are right, but where did these people go? Did they just evaporate?" I answered, "Ken, I really do not know, or can't even guess."

On the way back to the *Inn* we stopped at the church and found it in the same condition as elsewhere. Dust covered everything, the pulpit, pews, books, and floors. We left foot prints wherever we stepped and pondered how long they might last before being erased by the winds of time.

Finally we visited the grave of Haggis Frisbee, the author of the report about the missing village of Auralee in 1755. Standing before the marker, I said, "Aye, Haggis Frisbee, ye deserve a far, far better place than this, but ye shall always be in our hearts an honorable citizen of Auralee." The cemetery, once a beautifully landscaped and gardened spot, was now only a mass of headstones, nothing else.

We returned to camp, ate a light meal, and discussed our plans for tomorrow. By now it was obvious to all of us that further time here would produce little if any additional information. Penoaken, the Inn, and their world had vanished, it no longer existed. Once again it was like, *we opened the door and there was no one there.* It was time to go. We would leave Auralee for the last time early in the morning. At 5:00 AM we ate breakfast, finished loading our ponies, took a last long look at the Inn, and left. Lori was still having difficulty with words, but she managed, "Aye, Freddy and Kenny, it be so sad, but we be so grateful to be goen safely home."

Our return trip to Auralee was very somber, but at four o'clock we arrived at the old tree stump. Yes, through it all the old stump where Ken and I first found Auralee had survived unscathed. It brought back some good memories. This will be our farewell for we shall not be coming this way again.

Soon the East Bridge came into view and just beyond it stood Angus. We hurried our caravan across and did not look back. *Behind the bridge is yesterday, and it no longer exists. On this side is our today, our tomorrow, our forever.* We are all somewhat traumatized, but very pleased to be home.

****

When we neared Angus's house we were greeted by Jean, Heather, and Christine. We were exhausted; thus, after a light meal and a bunch of hugs and kisses, we went to our homes and told our wives we would tell them all about our venture in the morning. Before retiring, I gave Jean a great big loving kiss and told her how deep my love for her was. "Ever since the first time we met, I knew you were the only girl for me, and no matter what the future may bring, you will always be...*my lady*. I love you."

As worn out as I was Penoaken remained on my mind. How could that ungodly catastrophe ever have occurred? Why was it necessary? I supposed like all wars throughout history, *man* was not destined to live peacefully and in harmony with his fellow man. Too many Gods, too many agreements, too much machismo, too little patience and understanding.

****

Jean was asleep and by the light of my bedside candle I looked at her. She looked so beautiful and so peaceful. Finally I blew out my candle and at last deep sleep finally consumed me...*as though I would sleep forever.*

CHAPTER 20

AWAKENING

SLOWLY I awakened from my deep sleep. But things were dim, hazy, with almost no clarity. My first thoughts were, *what's the matter?* Shortly I began faintly to hear voices which were not understandable to me. Gradually things started to take on form and I scrambled to sort things out.

What is this place? A white room, a bed with white sheets, tubes in my nose and arms, a large vase full of colorful flowers on a white table beside my white bed. Was this heaven? Where is Jean?.... I faintly made out a group of three indistinct specters talking in tones indiscernible to me. One possibly was a nurse and the other two might possibly be Samantha and Ken. I managed to reason, they wouldn't be in heaven. Then, where is this place?

I tried to speak but all I could muster was a faint garbled whisper. I wheezed and coughed, "Where am I? Who are you? What's going on here? This is not Auralee, where's Jean?"

Eventually my efforts to speak became loud enough to gain the attention of the three specter-like apparitions. Then the first words I could understand were something like, "*Oh, my God, he is awake and trying to say something.*" The specter who could be a nurse ran to my bedside. I tried to speak again but the effort was too much for me; I collapsed back onto my pillows. Evidently the nurse had pushed an emergency alarm for shortly the room seemed full of green and blue clad uniforms without heads or hands; seemed nothing was in them. Then one of the uniforms spoke, "Doctor, come quick, he's trying to say something." Suddenly, the uniforms were taking me away. I was scared but later found out they were taking me to a recovery room. In my befuddled mind I thought to myself, *"Now I know where I am… I'm in a soap opera and all that is missing is the music and the drip, drip, drip.*

Over what seemed to be a couple of days my situation improved. I was considerably more lucent and aware of my surroundings. It was now possible for me to carry on abbreviated conversations with the uniforms that I now identified as doctors and nurses. Still I was extremely confused and realized for certain, *I am not in Auralee.*

As yet I had not received any answers as to where I was or how I got here, nor been allowed any visitors. The doctors kept me slightly sedated to give my mind and body more time to further recover. They started me on a little real food, if you could call it that, warm broths and some watery mashed potatoes.

After what seemed an eternity, I received my first visitors: mom, dad, and Sue Ellen, for about ten minutes. The next day it was Ken, Samantha, and my boss, Dan Clark. From them I learned a piece here and a piece there about my situation. At last my chief physician, Dr. Dan Finney, said I had regained some of my strength and stability and it was now appropriate for me to hear what had happened to me. A nurse and a nurse's aide pushed me in my wheelchair to a room with windows on three sides where I could see the outside world again. The sun was shinning brightly; it was a gorgeous day. Dr. Finney began:

****

"Fred, on a lovely day in late in March you were returning home from evidently a pleasure drive in the countryside when a truck swerved head on into your car's path. It was a catastrophic wreck. Your car was totaled and you, as well as the truck driver who was DUI, were critically injured.

"You were brought into the emergency room with very low vital signs. Frankly, Fred, you weren't expected to survive. At first your brain scan was relatively flat but from the beginning there was low level activity which very slowly began to increase. However, you remained unconscious and from the beginning you were placed on total life support. You remained that way for 2 weeks until ten days ago. Today my guarded prognosis is for almost a full recovery. Your physical condition is good, your broken ribs and leg are healing, and the trauma from your head injuries has diminished over time." When Dr. Finney finished, I slumped back in my wheelchair, stunned.

I never went to Scotland…no Penoaken, no Auralee, no Jean, Ken never left, no Heather. Everything and everyone was an absolute figment of a traumatic dream; I had never left Chicago. There had to be more to this. I must talk to Ken.

My mind totally rejected what Doctor Finney told me. My life in Auralee *was* real, and it *did* happen, I know it did and called out, "Jean, Jean, please come to me." *It was as if God had hit the delete key on my life's computer and sent it to the wastebasket…and now he had pressed the restore key. Suddenly my life was back where it all started.*

Over the course of the following two weeks my physical condition improved but mentally, in the doctors' opinions, I still refused to accept reality. I was placed in a private room, was eating easily digestible solid foods, walking for extending periods with the aid of a walker, and could have visitors for an hour or so each day.

On a daily basis I learned additional bits of information about my situation. There was Samantha, my job, Ken, but no Auralee, no Jean. That was the storyline, but I was still not buying into it… *Auralee exists somewhere.*

****

One morning they released the few personal effects to me that were recovered from my accident: my wallet and it's contents, a pair of shoes and socks, a damaged wrist watch, some keys, thirty cents in change, and nothing else. Something was missing!….. *The silver ring Jean had given me…where was it?* I immediately reported it missing but was informed nothing like a ring was recovered. *How could it not be there? Where was it?* Like the rest of Auralee it too was not real, only like a figment of my imagination.

****

In mid July I returned to my apartment and by now was able to get around without my walker. My life was beginning to return to what it used to be. I returned to work on a half day schedule and Sam was taking over my life as she had done before my accident.

I was once more not a happy camper and my life was fast becoming that familiar same old routine with little feeling or freedom and no personality. I reminded myself, *This is where it all started, and it was not going to again become my game plan. I will need to deal with this once more.*

As time crept onward my health continued to significantly improve, but my mind would not accept that which I was being told was reality when in my heart I knew it wasn't.

During my recovery I thanked Ken many, many times for being so attentive, and asked him for another favor. "Go with me to the park this evening." The same park where after returning from my first visit to Auralee I heard voices asking me to *come back to Auralee.* Ken naturally agreed to accompany me.

****

At the park we sat and I asked Ken, "Has anything unusual occurred to you since the day of my accident?" He responded, "Well, Fred, besides being concerned about you and missing you, no not really. Why do you ask?"

I replied, "Ken, listen closely for I have an amazing story to tell you, and if at any time you hear me say something that sounds familiar, or even if you only sense something, tell me immediately." He answered, "OK, ole buddy, I shall do that."

I began to relate our visit to Penoaken and Auralee. I told him of Jean, Heather, Tiffany, BJ, Angus, Lori, Henry, Scotty, and all the folks we met, and Ken you were there too. I told him of our experiences, his and mine, of finding Auralee, about our marriages, the golf course, our visits to Penoaken, the end of the world, and every little detail I could think of including his "inventing" Pizza. Ken's attention was always composed and total. When I finished he thoughtfully said, "God, Fred, what a story. You were very emotional, very compelling, and as you told it, utterly believable.

"To think it took place only during your coma is difficult for me to believe. And, you know, oddly at times I did get squeamish as if something you said seemed somehow to resonate with me." I continued, "Ken, trust me with this one…Heather and BJ are somewhere beyond the arc of time waiting for you." Ken squirmed a bit, but said nothing. Finally, I told Ken, "Have one more thing to do and you must be a part of it.

"The two of us must return to Scotland and retrace our visit to Penoaken and Auralee. We must have closure somehow." Ken studied thoughtfully for awhile before answering, "Oh, hell yes, Fred, there is no way I would miss this trip and I kinda hope we find Auralee. When do we leave?" I replied, "In a month or so, I just need a little more time."

****

With the anticipation of our trip, my mental and physical well being improved to the place where I felt up to our leaving for Scotland. I had everything here in good order except my relationship with Samantha. With her my life had returned to where it was prior to my accident. Same old country club, dinner, dancing, playing bridge, and listening to Sam and her crowd babble. She was still the self-centered, in charge, person she always was. In my "dream" we had reached a point of understanding that our relationship should end, and I had to arrive at that status again. I had so far resisted most aspects of a physical relationship with Sam as I was still married to Jean. And then there was Tiffany. Until it was proven otherwise, that was the way it would be.

****

Ken and I continued our daily talks about Auralee and our trip back to Scotland. This would be my final forte. Either we find Auralee and stay there, or if it would not be there, then Auralee must have been only a figment in my mind. Meanwhile Ken became very engrossed in our effort to locate Auralee; he was eager to begin our journey saying if we should find it and a girl by the name of Heather was waiting for him with a son named BJ, he would stay.

We selected late August for our departure date; when the date arrived and we boarded our flight, our anxieties, fears, and anticipations were all on fast forward. Fortunately our trip was smooth and uneventful, but nevertheless tiring. We landed, collected our bags, and looked around. I said to Ken, "Been here

before. It looks familiar, come on, let's go to the car rental area."
We went up the escalator, turned right past two baggage carousels
and stood before our counter. I looked at Ken said, "How's this
for knowing my way around?"

We loaded our baggage, got behind the wheel, Ken grabbed his
map, and started looking at it. I said, "Hey, ole buddy, don't
think you'll need that, but you can keep me honest." We quickly
departed the airport to the west and began to leave Edinburgh.
Ken commented, "So far you do seem to know your way around."
I replied, "Yes, Sir, like been here, done this. If my calculations
are correct we should be at Penoaken in around two hours. By
the way, Ken, if you notice anything which appears familiar, do
let me hear from you."

About two hours later we arrived at the turn-off to Penoaken
and exited the expressway. Soon we arrived at the boundary
to the village and immediately on our left, where it should be,
we noticed a large gateway and a driveway leading to a large
structure at the end.

The sign read *The Olde Inn*, not the *Travis Inn at Penoaken,* yet
this had to be the place. We parked near the entrance to the Inn
and entered via a massive front door which opened into a large
lobby area. Across the room was the reception desk and behind
it stood a comely looking lady who was...*definitely not Lori*. Ken
said, "Fred, are you sure this is the place?" I retorted, "God, Ken,
I think it is, it has to be."

As we walked toward the counter we passed *The Pub,* only now
it was called, of all things, *Inn Here*. I glanced inside; it was not
Scotty who was pouren the ale. I was beginning to ponder over
what was happening. Suddenly nothing seemed to be as it should
be.

I inquired from the manger, Mr. Duncan Tremont, about Lori
and Henry Travis. He replied that a few years ago times were

tough, they abandoned the Inn, disappeared, and nay been heard from since, a very strange occurrence. As there were no heirs, he purchased the Inn through a foreclosure procedure.

I thought, *Does that mean Henry, Lori, and Scotty are still in Auralee?* Our first clue! We were hopeful they might be there, and that soon we would be able to verify it. After we checked in, a young bellhop took our bags and led us to our rooms.

During the afternoon of August 11th we made plans for our venture. We drove north on a narrow path where hopefully at the end we would find the meadow where we had parked before, and gratefully, it was there. I said to Ken, "OK, this is where we will come in the morning," and pointing due east said, "head that away."

At 10:00 AM on the 12th we had everything loaded and drove to our starting point, the meadow, and at eleven o'clock put on our backpacks and began walking east. Anticipation was high and if all went well, the distance to the old tree stump would be a little over seven miles which should take us from 4 to 6 hours.

At 1:30 PM we lunched and estimated we had covered around three miles. Slow going but we had to be careful; so far I had not seen anything familiar. At 2:15 we resumed our trek. By 5:00 it would be dark; we would need to have our camp established before then. In next hour we covered another mile, still over three miles to go, and only a couple hours of daylight left. I suggested that since there would be 9 hours of daylight available to us on the 13th, we find a place to camp and retire for the night. Though it was densely wooded, we occasionally could peek through the foliage and catch a glimpse of a star and the glimmer of a little moonlight. These were good signs that tomorrow would be clear.

We awoke at 6:00 AM on the 13th, hurried through breakfast, loaded our backpacks, and were on our way at 6:45. A check of our compasses confirmed we were still on an easterly heading. By 10:30 I estimated we should be in the area where we had found the old tree stump on our last two trips. But nothing familiar was in sight.

No stump, no crooked tree, landmarks we had seen on our last trips, were found. We elected to split up and search further. Ken would circle to the north and west. I would go south and east and we would meet in an hour and a half. We piled up a stack of rocks to identify our location and left our packs.

It was very quiet in the forest. An occasional bird and rustling leaves were the only sounds. After a couple hours we'd covered our chartered courses twice. We had found nothing at all unusual and no trace of anything familiar. It was afternoon and after we took a break for some food and rest, I suggested to Ken we must be near the right place, but we should move east another half mile and redo our circle. At 2:00 PM we moved out and by 4:30 we had completed our objectives but still found nothing. I was becoming concerned and told Ken we again had to set up camp as it would soon be dark and offered, "Perhaps tonight something may occur."

The night passed without an incident. Several times I tried calling out, "Angus, we are here, Freddy and Kenny. We have returned to Auralee." Only silence prevailed and soon daylight returned.

We agreed to spend the 14th attempting to locate anything we could recognize. Again we split up and combed a circular route around our camp. Noon came, passed, and afternoon bore no better results. It was now down to tonight. If we found nothing, I would have to matter-of-factly recognize that Auralee was nothing more than a manifestation of my imagination.

The night was painfully long and I did not find sleep. As the darkness passed and daylight returned, I was absolutely devastated having been so certain we'd find Auralee; we had not.

I was noticeably sobbing. Finally, I turned to Ken and said, "OK, Ken, let's pack up and go. In my mind I clearly see Auralee, and hear everyone but they have abandoned me. Yet, I will not accept that Auralee and Jean are not real. They are out there somewhere in time *Beyond the Arc* and someday I'll find them." Ken looked at me saying, "Fred, I am so sorry for you. I'd give my right arm to have found our Auralee; but, now I must agree it's time go home, we'll not find her here today."

****

We packed our gear and began the journey back to Penoaken, arriving there at 4:30 PM on the 15th. That evening we confirmed our return flight to Chicago for the following afternoon.

The next morning we drove to Edinburgh and boarded our plane for the USA. For the duration we said very little. Neither of us knew how to express our disappointments; we never even had a martini. Finally as we were landing I said, "Ken, thank you, my dearest friend. I just could not have made it there and back without you." He answered, "Fred, I am glad I was with you. I know this has been a crushing disappointment for you. I for one won't give up hope and I know you won't either, *perhaps, someday, somehow.*"

CHAPTER 21

AFTERWARD

BEFORE WE left for Scotland my attorneys filed a large lawsuit against the trucking firm whose intoxicated driver caused my injury, seventy million after taxes, medical, and attorney costs. A huge sum, but God knows, I suffered plenty, and in more ways than one. If I had found Auralee I would have gladly left the award to my folks. Since I did not find her, the money would be used to secure a golf and ski resort in northern Wisconsin, an area which reminded me of the Scottish Highlands. The name would be *The Inn at Auralee*. In February 2009 the judgment was awarded by the jury in the full amount of my claim, and requests by the defense for a retrial were denied by the courts.

I suggested to Ken that he quit his job as I did mine, and accept the title of Senior Vice-President of the resort. After considerable thought, he graciously accepted my offer. Next I hired a major firm from Milwaukee to search out locations for consideration, some place in or near mountains with a lake, a golf course, and skiing. It should not be the most pretentious place, but one large enough to offer quiet relaxation, away from the rat race of twenty-first century culture.

Our firm located a spot for sale in northern Wisconsin; thus, we made our first visit to assure the resort was what we wanted for a price which could be negotiated. Arriving at the resort we were instantaneously impressed. Even the weather was sunny and pleasant.

We drove directly to the office of Mr. James Moore, the owner and general manager, who warmly welcomed us and took us to a beautifully decorated conference room. In addition to Ken, myself, Frank Hurst from the firm, *Traveling Locations*, my attorney, and our traveling secretary, present were Mr. Moore's chief accountant, Alice Fromm, and his attorney, George Maletti. The atmosphere was cordial and after appropriate introductions Mr. Moore began a slide show presentation. Following the show, he asked if we would like to take a physical tour of the resort area. We agreed, and left in one of his custom vans.

The tour of the 72 acre facility took six hours including a brief stop for lunch at the resort restaurant where we were introduced to Chef Felix Conte. The food was excellently prepared and presented. It was impressive and at the conclusion of our tour told Mr. Moore we would discuss our findings and get back to him soon.

All my people were impressed and I asked my firm *Traveling Locations* to proceed with a formal inspection of the resort's plant and get an opinion of our financial opportunities. Moore's asking price was 62 million dollars. What we had seen was impressive.

Golf: On property a 9 hole executive course, par 30. An 18 hole championship course within a half mile with special times and rates for resort guests.

Skiing: On property 2 runs with snow making capability, one student and one intermediate. Larger skiing runs were located within four miles and had special rates and times for resort guests.

<u>Hiking and Fishing</u>: Shaded walking paths throughout property and major hiking trails nearby. The resort had a 3 acre lake for small boats, swimming and fishing, during winter ice fishing.

<u>Other recreational opportunities</u>: Lighted volley ball, croquette, and tennis courts. Duplicate and social bridge games, birding tours, and game rooms for the younger set including a teen club.

<u>Restaurants</u>: Resort dining room and cocktail lounge, all inclusive breakfast buffet, bar and grill at the golf course and ski facilities.

All rooms were spacious and large suites were available. Each room was equipped with satellite TV, telephone, computer connections, and special perks.

We needed to await the appraisers report on the resort's plant and for the financial reports. They were expected to be available in about three weeks. Meantime Ken and I would give our thoughts to staff. I planned no big change in staff and would encourage them to remain.

When the reports arrived, as hoped, they were quite good, excellent even, and I was relieved. After due analysis I said, "Hey gang, this looks great; it is just what I wanted. Let's put together an offer and I want it to be a very fair offer, no low-balling, OK?" Everyone agreed, so our team went to work and immediately set a date with Mr. Moore and his folks for early Tuesday, April 7th.

On that day we arrived and were welcomed graciously and ushered to the President's office where coffee and Danish were waiting for us. After appropriate small talk, I took the podium and said, "President Moore, your asking price of sixty-two million dollars for the resort, all buildings and physical properties is a reasonable beginning. Therefore, I will counter with what I hope will meet your expectations:
"I offer to close within 30 days, if that meets with your timetable, and my offer is 56 million dollars." I noticed Moore and his

associates never flinched and took it as a positive sign. They asked for a break in order to discuss the offer, and we retired to the dining room to wait.

I said, "Well, seems like a good start." After about an hour Moore asked us to return and he said, "Fred, this is a good offer, but I will need 2 million more." I replied, without counsel, "Hell, Jim, sounds fair to me." Without hesitation, he stuck out his hand and replied, "It's a deal. It looks as if you are the owner of a fine resort in northern Wisconsin." Not exactly what my team had expected, but I told them later that I wasn't in the mood to quibble. It's a done deal, let's move on.

The closing on April 22nd went well. The resort staff had all agreed to continue with us and that pleased me. The only changes would be in what we would call things. The resort would now be, *The Inn at Auralee*, the dining room, *The Penoaken Room*, and the cocktail lounge, *The Pub*.

****

My one remaining need was to sever permanently my relationship with Samantha, and I reasoned my approach to her would need to be brief, to the point, and as delicately put as possible. I called Sam and asked her to meet me later this evening at the country club cocktail lounge as I was flying back to Chicago and had something to discuss with her. She noted I sounded serious and I replied it was important. I thought, *I remember during my coma I severed my ties with Sam, but she did not share in this experience.*

That evening when she arrived I already had a glass of her favorite red wine waiting. I stood and said, "Good evening, Sam. You look marvelous as usual, please sit down as I have a toast to propose." Sam replied, "Thank you, Fred. You sound so gallant. I love toasts." To myself I thought, *Well OK, but I am not certain about this one.* Anyway I continued, "To your good health, to your continued enjoyment of life, and to the memories of all the fun times we have enjoyed together. I shall always remember them fondly." We each took a sip of wine and I could see a look of discomfort overtaking her.

I continued, "Sam, I am saying goodbye. It is with a high degree of sorrow I do this, but Ken and I have resigned our jobs and are permanently moving to Wisconsin. I think both of us know our continued togetherness would only lead to unhappiness on both our parts. So goodbye, Sam, and may the future treat you with respect and prosperity." I took a large slug of my wine and waited.

Sam sat, calmly sipping her wine for a few moments. Then she looked at me, and answered, "Fred, I'm sorry about this, but it does not come as a surprise. I have noticed a change in you ever since you recovered from your accident. It has been like you never really returned to us. To me your life has been, well, like, you are someplace else.

"Thus, reluctantly, I accept your goodbye. I wish you and Ken good fortune, and hope you will both be happy with whatever you do." I thought her response extremely surprising, but decided to just quietly accept what I very much considered a good result. With that, Sam stood up, turned, and strode out of the club and I hoped out of my life.

Later when I related my conversation to Ken, he commented, "God, Fred, the end of the world must be near. *Didn't you do this before* or am I just dreaming?" I gave his reply a very studied reply. "Yes, Ken, I did do this before during my so-called comatic dream, but you and Samantha were not really there." He replied, "Well, okay, ole buddy, *but something seems familiar to me.*"

I said nothing to Ken about his reply, but it carried with it a most intriguing thought, *a solid indication that he does recall something which occurred in my dream.*

CHAPTER 22

AT LAST PEACE

WELL, I told myself, *That does it for Samantha and Chicago.* Before I left I invited my folks and siblings to visit me at the Inn, but I doubted they would do it; perhaps Sue Ellen might. For awhile it seemed rather wonderfully strange to have all that behind me. However, major things were not right. Auralee was gone and that included Jean and Tiffany and all the gang.

Officially at the Inn everything seemed to be business as usual; I knew I had to keep myself active and moving toward some objective or I would go nuts. Finally, it came to me, I would recreate the Village of Auralee…. Yes, right here at the Inn…and I had the spot. A three and one-half acre plot complete with a small stream that ran down the east boundary.

In early May I committed a local builder to recreate Auralee. It would have replicas of the home of Angus Macgregor, the home of Jean and Freddy Mitchell, the croft of Heather Crawford Effington including the corral complete with 2 Shetland ponies, 4 sheep, and her sheep dog, Candy. In the center of the square a one-half scale fountain would flow like the one in Scotland.

Other buildings would include the kirk, the bakery, a barn, and at least two other residential homes.

At the far east end of the village there would be a stone bridge which crossed the small stream to a wooded area where a large weather beaten tree stump would be placed. The village and all the surrounding area would be constructed to be as much like Auralee as possible. In the center of the square there would be a flag pole displaying the Scottish white cross on a field of blue flapping gallantly in the breeze.

It took only three months for completion and I was extremely pleased with the outcome. This gave me some solace. On weekends and holidays the village, staffed by people dressed in mid-eighteenth century Scottish attire, was open to resort guests and the public. The Elder of Auralee was a gentleman called Angus. Guests were carried, if they wished, along the streets in authentic small carts by ponies named America and Illinois. Auralee was a tremendous hit with the guests and public.

Ken and I spent many evenings on our stump talking and reminiscing. Ken had become more certain there was a meaning to my story, and one evening he volunteered, "Perhaps Auralee is more than only an illusion."

We worried as our government leaders continued to cram us full of all-is-well propaganda. Yet, we knew their ravings were not well intended. To believe otherwise, now that would truly be a dream. As it had been for some time, the world continued to cascade toward oblivion. I said to Ken, "Damn it, our visit to Auralee was more than a dream, it was a harbinger of the future."

****

On December 1, 2009 Ken took a couple weeks vacation to visit his old haunts in Chicago. He was to return by no later than December 14th in order to be here for the Christmas rush. I asked him to say hello to Sammy and to not invite her for a visit. He laughed and agreed.

When Ken had not returned by December 16th I began to worry and started calling some of his old pals. They all told me the same thing...Ken left Chicago on December 13th for Wisconsin. Having heard nothing from him I advised authorities of the possibility of a missing person. They took my information, told me they would look into the matter and advise me of any findings. I was worried beyond worry; this did not at all fit Ken's profile.

The police reported they found Ken's car but other than that they found nothing unusual about his disappearance. They simply did not have a clue as to where he might have gone. Couldn't help but think perhaps, perhaps...*Auralee*. Was it possible? Then considered, *no...why would he go there without me?*

On December 19th I temporarily replaced Ken as my Senior Vice-President. I missed him badly and hoped somehow he would just show up, but I began to have doubts. Fortunately the holiday season was going well. The Inn was full and that kept me occupied. I received another report from the police, but it was of little help. They asked me to send someone to pick up Ken's car, which I did.

On December 23rd I hosted the Little Christmas Eve dance and dinner. It was a very festive occasion. We booked a dance band from Chicago that specialized in the big band sound. Dinner included roast turkey, glazed ham, all the trimmings and unlimited Champagne.

Christmas eve was cold, crisp, but sunny, and for many it was a day of quiet recovery from all the festivities of the previous evening. A light snow had fallen to aid Santa on his quest and my thoughts returned to early childhood Christmases with my family and to Auralee, with Jean, Tiffany, and all the gang. I wanted to ask Santa for just one great big present, to be with Jean.

****

Christmas morning arrived, a carbon copy of the day before. As I reached for my clock to turn off the alarm I was suddenly taken aback…. *On the pinky of my left hand was a small silver ring… the ring Jean had given me!* I was startled and pulled my hand back, put on my glasses and stared at it. My body was jolted by a strange tingling sensation…. *How did the ring get here? Where had it been? What does it mean?* Again I looked at my ring. Suddenly, realizing, *yes, it must be!* The answer seemed obvious…. I must with all haste *personally* return the ring to Jean. It was my passport home to Auralee. But how would I get there? That was the part which was not obvious to me, but knew there had to be an answer.

Later in the morning I visited my stump in the wooded area near my little village. It was a magnificent white Christmas and everything at the resort was perking along well. At around 11 o'clock I sat down and could not help but think once more of Angus telling me, *"If ye want somethen strongly enough it could happen."*

I looked at my little silver ring, rubbed it, and said, *"Little ring, if there was ever a wish that you could grant me it is to take me home. Home to Auralee, to Jean and to Tiffany, for I am so very lost and so want to be with them."*

I tearfully sat thinking about how distraught I felt to not be with Jean and Tiffany for Christmas and could well imagine their unhappiness. Yet as hard as I wished it, the only indication anything would change lay with my ring. As I looked hopefully at it and rubbed it, my mind slowly wandered into a state of half-sleep.

Sometime later as I began to awaken and my mind ever so slowly returned to the present…yet something seemed not exactly as I had left it. My stump was here, but the concrete walk which led from the bridge to the stump was now only a narrow dirt path. and there was a faint sound of water coursing over rocks…. Now fully awake, my pulse was racing…. I looked at my watch and it was exactly *seven minutes past noon on Christmas Day.* My thoughts jumped out at me…. *The gate is open, dummy, the gate is open! It must be that…May 15th in Auralee has matched December 25th here in Wisconsin.*

****

Breathing hard I began walking then running, toward the little stone bridge and crossed it. Suddenly winter had turned to spring and standing in front of me was Angus. I was in a state of shock and the feeling was beyond comprehension. It exceeded emotion, euphoric did not begin to describe it. The feeling was spiritual as though this occasion had always been ordained.

I was weak but managed to rush to Angus and almost knocked him down in my eagerness to hug him and said, "Angus, I am home and this time forever. Please, Sir, I love you, please take me home to Jean and Tiffany."

Angus said, "Aye, Freddy, lad. We always knew you'd come home to us and Kenny already be here." That startled me, but after my initial reaction it just wasn't all that much of a surprise. And here I was worrying about him all this time. Angus had his cart; thus, the trip home only took about 25 minutes. When we entered the village my heart took off like a locomotive under full steam.

I simply could not hide my anxiety, and Angus said, "Be ye ready for a real homecoming, Freddy. Ye see we knew ye be comen." I responded, "Huh?" Angus replied, "Aye, laddy, we knew. In the Highlands o' ole Scotland, we ha' our ways o' knowen these things."

When Angus's house appeared I noticed a small crowd of people standing in front of it, as if they were expecting me. And as we approached they became identifiable: Jean, Tiffany, Ken, Heather, BJ, John, Mary, Henry, Lori, Scotty, Christine, and Reverend Dundee. I thought, *But how could they have known and just be here awaiting my arrival?* They looked just as I had last seen them. Then I realized, never mind *this be the Highlands of ole Scotland.* God, I will never understand any of this; what a fantastic trip it has been!

The cart stopped, no before the cart stopped, I leaped from it, ran to Jean, threw my arms about her and we kissed enthusiastically. I then picked Tiffany up and kissed her too. Everyone was crying. Jean struggled, "Oh, Freddy, dinna ye leave us again. I be so fearful" I said, "No Jean, my love, this time is forever. I shan't be leaving again."

Ken stepped forward and said, "What kept ye ole buddy? I have been here a couple of weeks." I just smiled and hugged him saying, "I love you, guy." Everyone else offered me their welcomes and I hugged or kissed every one of them. I was so unabashedly happy. Reverend Dundee stepped forward saying, "Laddy, ye and Kenny gave us a real scare. I be hard pressed to provide answers worth tellen. But we citizens o' Auralee be accustomed to keepen our faith that all will turn out to be as it should...and it has."

Soon I got around to asking Ken how he managed to get here, since at the time of his trip to Chicago, he still wasn't sure he had been here before. He replied with his usual casualness, "Oh, heck, it was easy. One minute I was driving down the highway returning to Wisconsin when suddenly everything went blank like I had just turned off my TV set. The next thing I knew I was sitting on that damn tree stump near the East Bridge and Angus was standing just across it. I got up, finally convinced that I had truly been here before and walked across it. That's it, ole buddy. Except, never figured to get here without you."

Ken continued, "It became clearly obvious I had been here before and seemed as if I had never been gone. My school, your medical clinic, the golf course were all here and familiar to me."

****

Everything in Auralee seemed to be prospering. To Ken and to me everything was the same as though we had never left and that was a very comforting feeling. Even the ponies, America, Illinois, and Heather's sheep dog, Candy, all acknowledged our returns with enthusiasm.

That first night as Jean and I lay close together I told her of my finding her ring on my finger Christmas morning and asked, "Jean, how did the ring find me?"

She smiled coyly, "Aye, Freddy, I dinna know, but ye remember I told thee that if ye ever be lost the ring willa bring ye back to me. That ha' always been ordained since I be given the ring by Reverend Dundee, thee Elder. I tell ye only God has for certain thee answer. We must trust in our faith, and remember, *here in the Highlands of ole Scotland anything be possible.*"

EPILOGUE

TIME GRACIOUSLY continued to pass in Auralee and we no longer made much reference to the twenty-first century. Each day here was now just an extension of our present life. Each day had sixty minutes in each hour, 24 hours in a day, 365 days in a year and so on.

Our memories of our *last life* continued to grow dimmer and dimmer, but we occasionally reflected on our travels in the *4th dimension, beyond the arc of time*. Why were we chosen for this? We would probably never know, but consider that the world we once were a part of, was in my dream destroyed. Civilization had devoured itself riding on the backs of deceit, hypocrisy, greed, hate, and lust for power. The desires of people who wished for a better world vanished and were blown away into oblivion by the *winds of time*. Even though our twenty-first century world does still exist, in my dream where our alter egos exist, there is a harbinger of what is to come.

One evening Ken said, "Fred, we, Lori, Henry, and Scotty are here in Glen Auralee...why us? I thought for awhile and responded. Ken, my gut feeling is...*There are lots, perhaps millions of other places like Auralee out there in the universe of God's house.* Didn't *he* say something like "*In my house of many rooms I have prepared one for you?*"

Perhaps, this is one of those rooms? What do you think, ole buddy." Ken responded, "Sounds like a good rationale to me, Fred, you always seem to come up with the big ones." I said, "Thanks, Ken, I think."

****

We returned to our respective homes. I kissed Jean, tucked Tiffany into bed, and said, "I love you both so dearly. Goodnight, bonnie Jean, goodnight, dearest Tiffany. I'll see you both tomorrow...in the glorious light of morning."

Somewhere in time, beyond the Arc...
in this place called Auralee.

BIBLIOGRAPHY

1...SCOTLAND, R. CONRAD STEIN, CHILDREN'S PRESS, A DIVISION OF SCHOLASTIC, INC. NEW YORK, NEW YORK, 2001

2...SCOTLAND, WILLIAM W. LACE, LUCENT BOOKS, SAN DIEGO, CALIFORNIA, 2001

3...WILLIAM WALLACE, GRAEME MORTON, SUTTON PUBLISHING, GREAT BRITAIN, 2001

4...WILLIAM WALLACE, BRAVE HEART, JAMES MACKAY, MAINSTREAM PUBLISHING, EDINBURGH AND LONDON, 1995

5...EVERYDAY LIFE IN RENAISSANCE ENGLAND, EMERSON, KATHY LYNN, WRITER'S DIGEST BOOKS, CINCINNATI, OHIO, 1996

ABOUT THE AUTHOR

THIS BOOK is a departure from Mitchell's previous historical fiction books which combines the concept of time travel with actual historical events. Although still traveling in time to a past era, Beyond the Arc is truly a fictional novel.

Mitchell, student of military history was, during the centennial years 1961-1965, Vice President of the Chicago Civil War Round Table, a prestigious gathering of authors and historians.

When asked during an interview why he chose to deviate from his past writings, responded, "Because I always wanted to do this book."

Mitchell is a native Illinoisan and a retiree from the old Bell Telephone System. He and his wife, Shirley, have resided in Arizona since his retirement in 1984.

ABOUT THIS BOOK

IN THE Highlands of ole Scotland at twelve AM on May 15th of each year a wee place called Auralee reappears from the mist of time. No mention of this place is mentioned in any maps or record...except for a brief notation in the journal of a small church in the village of Penoaken.

The record states in the year of our Lord, 1754, a place called Auralee disappeared without a trace. Come along on this incredible journey back in time, and find much more than you had anticipated.

OTHER BOOKS BY THE AUTHOR

When Rivers Meet, Vantage Press,2005
The Hindenburg's Farewell, Trafford Publishing, 2006
December 7,1941, Trafford Publishing, 2008